Love on
Life
Support

No matter what,
there is Hope!
Romans 15:13

Deb & Bruce
Rem

Endorsements

Bruce and Deb Potts have two of the biggest hearts for Jesus and for marriage we have ever seen. They have led a marriage mentoring ministry that has helped save countless marriages. This captivating novel will give you a glimpse into their soul, and you will not only meet a couple deeply in love, but a couple on God's mission to reach the world through marriage God's way.

—Dave and Ann Wilson, Co-Hosts of *Family Life Today*

Love On Life Support is a tender and harrowing story of the gloriously layered and ruddy nature of marriage, faith, and life. Readers are taken on an intimate journey through the peaks and valleys of a Christian marriage that outwardly appears strong, but inwardly is shattered. Deb and Bruce illuminate the restorative and redemptive thread of faith that is continuously needed throughout life to pull the broken pieces back together. This authentic, and at times uncomfortable glimpse into the deep divides within marriage, is a powerful reminder of our need to forgive and be forgiven, and to continually draw deeper in our surrender to Jesus, to better serve one another.

—Michael and Gina Kell Spehn, *NY Times*-Bestselling authors of *The Color of Rain* and Founders, New Day Foundation for Families

Through the power of story, my friends, Bruce and Deb Potts, have beautifully communicated timeless truths about relationships that are sure to add tremendous value to your life and marriage. I trust their words because I trust them.

—Christopher Cook, podcast host of *Win Today with Christopher Cook* and author

This story is a vivid portrayal of a marriage in crisis that is transformed by faith. The semi-autobiographical nature of this novel makes it unique—and powerful. One wouldn't expect a relationship-focused novel to be a suspenseful page-turner, but this one is! It is also realistic in ways that will help readers learn and grow in their own marriage. I'm delighted to recommend this fascinating novel.

—**Shaunti Feldhahn**, social researcher and best-selling author of *For Women Only* and *For Men Only*

Deb and Bruce Potts have spent a lifetime learning about marriage and helping couples. Now they've found a new, creative way to package all that wisdom. Set against the backdrop of the eerie, early days of a worldwide pandemic, this story is a reminder that if we were to see our marriage from every angle, we'd see more clearly than ever our own contribution to its thriving or dying—and we might even take more responsibility for how we're growing up and showing up.

—**Kelly Flanagan**, best-selling author of *The Unhiding of Elijah Campbell*

Love on Life Support is ideal for Christian couples or individuals who are struggling and cannot or will not pursue outside help. It's also encouraging for ALL couples who want to remember and rekindle what drew them together and aid in taking steps toward one another again. An engaging read and full of interesting real-life detail.

—**Karen G. Shive**, MA, LPC, Marriage therapist and speaker

If you need to know, unequivocally, that God is with you—even through the most difficult times, then this book is for you. As I read this story, I was deeply moved by the eloquently written metaphors revealing the restorative presence and power of God and how to receive His love. This is an emotional love story that took me on an all too familiar journey of how relying on prayer, even in my work as a therapist, is a way to access every day miracles and the redemptive love of God.

—Sheela E. Wright, Clinical Therapist and Marriage Mentor

Bruce and Deb Potts are real people. They have lived nearly all the ups and downs that life can throw a person's way. They love people deeply and want them to live beautifully. And they know that every life and every marriage hits walls that are near to impossible to climb over, especially when our strength seems to fail.

I have watched Bruce and Deb invest their lives in people and in their marriages, helping to build stronger foundations that can weather the storms that build over time and those hurricanes that crash upon us when least expected.

One thing I know about marriage and about life; everyone falters and everyone needs encouragement and support. And everyone finds that their own resources, at some point, run dry. I am so thankful for the Potts's committing their lives to see that married couples aren't alone and stuck only to their own ingenuity. Read on and find inspiration for your own marriage journey!!

—Steve Andrews, Co-Founder, Kensington Church

With inspiring honesty and refreshing joy, Bruce and Deb share a story that goes to the heart of so many marriages. From the thrill of new relationship to the darkness of personal trial, there are crossroads at every season. And through it all, we are reminded of community, humility, and connection to the Love that helps us love others.

—Chris Cook, Director of Care Initiatives, Kensington Church

Have you ever wondered what it was like for families in trauma during COVID? I knew several families in the situation where a spouse was in ICU and the other spouse couldn't even go in at all. It was hard to watch, but I'd always wondered what it was like. Now, because of *Love on Life Support*, I have a better idea! The book is based on the true-life story of Bruce and Deb Potts but written as fiction. As you read, you'll feel their pain and experience some behind-the-scenes stories and emotions that may surprise you. Grab your copy today for inspiration to love more, live life full out, and trust the amazing God who heals, renews and restores both bodies and marriages. Bravo!

—Marnie Swedberg, Mentor to Millions

Brimming with wisdom—relational, spiritual, emotional—*Love on Life Support* is an invitation to deeper intimacy with God and your spouse. Throughout my work with struggling couples, the common denominator of all success stories is HOPE. *Love on Life Support* offers couples the hope of Jesus and provides a beautiful illustration that with God all things are possible—even the miraculous healing of a broken marriage.

—Tammy Moore, Director of Marriage Initiatives, Kensington Church

Fairy tale weddings rarely end up in happy marriages unless couples do the work. It is work that can only be done with God. When we go to Him in frustration, He never points the finger at our spouse. Instead, He shines the light on our own imperfections and ask us to change. Submitting to His wisdom and guidance, the marriage foundation is strengthened for the inevitable storms of life. For Chris and Amy, when a Category 5 crisis hits, it is almost too late. But God ...

Deb and Bruce Potts have written a beautiful story, a tale not rooted in the enchantment of fantasy, but a real-life marriage on the rocks. It is full of God's wisdom and sure to bring abundant hope and joy to every reader's marriage.

—Jeff & Gina Petherick, Marriage Mentors

Love on Life Support

Deb and Bruce Potts

ELK LAKE PUBLISHING INC.

PUBLISHING THE POSITIVE
Plymouth, Massachusetts

A Christian Company
ElkLakePublishingInc.com

Copyright Notice

Love on Life Support

Cover and Interior Design: Derinda Babcock, Deb Haggerty

Editor(s): Sue Fairchild, Cristel Phelps, Deb Haggerty

PUBLISHED BY: Elk Lake Publishing, Inc., 35 Dogwood Drive, Plymouth, MA 02360, 2022

Library Cataloging Data

Names: Potts, Deb and Bruce (Deb and Bruce Potts)

Love on Life Support / Deb and Bruce Potts

266 p. 23cm × 15cm (9in × 6 in.)

ISBN-13: 978-1-64949-768-0 (paperback) | 978-1-64949-769-7 (trade hardcover) | 978-1-64949-770-3 (trade paperback) | 978-1-64949-771-0 (e-book)

Key Words: Contemporary Christian Fiction; Medical Fiction Romance; Second-Chance Inspirational Fiction; Small Town Fiction; Marriage Reconciliation Romance; Flawed Characters; Hope

Library of Congress Control Number: 2022951291 Fiction

Dedication

To our readers' pursuits of storybook marriages. May you all become soul mates and kindred spirits who weave your hearts together through threads of both adversity and wonder—just as Abba imagined.

Consider it pure joy, my brothers and sisters, whenever you face trials of many kinds, because you know that the testing of your faith produces perseverance. Let perseverance finish its work so that you may be mature and complete, not lacking anything. —James 1:2–4

Acknowledgments

We've often read in book acknowledgments that many people are behind the writing and publishing of a book. And now we understand just how important those people are.

We are thankful for the Marriage Initiatives at Kensington Church in Orion, Michigan. Our leaders, Sid and the late Nino Pecoraro, welcomed us to that ministry and trained us to lead in their place when they moved on to other pursuits. We learned to love and do life with our mentees from Nino and Sid.

We developed a great appreciation for Peter Scazzero's book, *Emotionally Healthy Spirituality*. Bruce and his small group worked through this material just before the pandemic and brain surgeries. That material was the inspiration for the Bible study in our story. Highly recommended!

We want to acknowledge the support and patience of our entire extended family as we toiled on this project well past the point when it seemed like a good idea to them.

The members of Bruce's medical team were irreplaceable experts and supportive encouragers. We especially want to thank Dr. Dashnaw (his neurosurgeon), and his Physician's Assistants (PAs): Michelle Strzelczk, Terri Jones, and Stephanie Martz. They and many other nurses, doctors, and frontline workers at William Beaumont Hospital in Troy,

Michigan, were dedicated in their care and improvisation during the biggest surge of COVID-19. This was a time when visitors were not allowed, so some of them graciously used their own cell phones to enable contact between Bruce and Deb.

Our thanks go to Joann Cooper, a lifelong friend and lover of Christian romance who graciously provided input as she read an advanced copy.

Amy Heidel, a neurosurgical PA and family friend, reviewed and polished the medical terminology. Thank you, Amy.

Bruce's miraculous recovery, which inspired this book, would not have occurred without the many people who prayed on our behalf. They are too numerous to list here. You know who you are! Thank you from the bottom of our hearts.

Finally, we must thank Jesus. The first half of our marriage was very similar to Chris and Amy's. We most certainly would have experienced the drift and decay they did if not for the miraculous timing of our meeting Jesus. We are grateful beyond words for the radical and welcome changes God brought into our marriage.

Prologue

Amy ended the call with shaking hands, then dropped her cell phone in her lap. She felt adrift, cut off from Chris, her husband and anchor. Panic crushed her as she envisioned the worst. Her imagination took over, filling her mind with tragic scenarios. She wailed, feeling helpless and hopeless.

I need you now, God. Help me! How much more can I endure?

Minutes passed, each one bringing more painful laments. She had never felt as alone or terrified. A worldwide pandemic confined them—Chris in an ICU and her at home alone. He was unreachable now, unable to speak or comprehend what was happening. He was in the hands of strangers, and his life hung in the balance.

Worst of all, the last time the two of them were together, they were both so angry they raged at each other. They hadn't even slept in the same bed.

She curled up on the love seat in a heap, sobs racking her body. She cried and cried until no more tears came. Then she just lay there, numb and broken.

Terrifying thoughts relentlessly tormented her. *What if he doesn't make it? I'll never see him or talk to him ever again.*

No, please God—no! I couldn't bear it. After all we've been through, this can't be the end. But … what if it is?

When Love Flourished— Twenty-Nine Years Ago

Chris watched Amy, her mom, and sister step out the front door to meet him. Amy's soft auburn hair was braided around her head, and her hazel eyes sparkled. She hugged him, then twirled. "I love when you plan adventurous dates. I can't wait to see where we're going today. Remember when you took me whitewater rafting that first time?"

He did remember. She'd been so scared and had even fallen out of the raft. He'd felt his stomach drop when he'd looked back in the raft, and she'd been gone. Jumping in, he'd come to her rescue. He remembered telling her, "You're doing great, Amy. Roll onto your back ... point your feet downstream ... toes out of the water. I'm right here with you. Breathe in the trough of the waves. Breathe ... breathe. Okay, you're okay. Hunter will slow down for us to catch up. Hunter will get us back in the boat."

And their guide had.

But seconds later, Hunter had yelled above the roar. "This is going to be dangerous. We're way off course. Lock your feet!"

As the raft entered the rapids, it rode sideways up the side of a rock at an extreme angle. A few more seconds, and it would flip, tossing everyone into the perilous current. There would be five swimmers and no one to rescue them.

"Everyone, lean into the high side." Hunter had used the oar on that side to push off the rock while he paddled with the other oar to rotate the raft. But the raft would not budge. "Lean! Lean!"

The raft teetered there for an instant while the thunderous water convulsed around them. Finally, the low side began to track downstream, pulling the raft flat again and allowing them all to return to their seats.

A day they'd never forget. And he hoped today would be another day they'd hold on to forever.

He watched from the porch as Amy bounced to the car like that raft upon the waves.

When she was out of earshot, Chris whispered to Amy's mom. "See you later, right?" He glanced at Amy's sister and held his index finger to his lips. Turning, he followed Amy to the car.

They buckled in, and he backed out of the driveway, feeling the satisfying rumble of his Camaro IROC-Z beneath him. "Settle back and enjoy the ride. I don't think you've ever been to this town before. We'll have lunch when we get there." He checked his pocket. *Yep, still there.* He took his hand away before she could notice. Their favorite cassette started playing, and she sang along in a rich alto voice. Three whole years of knowing and loving Amy gave him a feeling of contentment he'd never known before. He couldn't wait to share this day with her in the little town of Rochester, Michigan.

She waited until he parallel parked on Main Street, then jumped out. "I'm glad you're driving. I don't think I'll ever be able to parallel park." She glanced up and down the street. "I've never been here before, but I'm looking forward to exploring."

He took her hand, and they walked down one side of Main Street, then up the other.

He thought again to that night after their whitewater trip and how he'd taken Amy's hand. He'd held his finger to his lips and pointed to a path leading away from the campsite. It felt good to be on solid ground with her at his side in the cool air, looking up to the countless stars in the black sky.

After they'd walked for a few minutes, Amy had stopped and faced him. "Chris McGrath, why did you jump in after me?"

He'd given her a wry half-smile. "Why do you think?"

She'd sighed. "Well, thank you for caring enough to protect me."

He'd pulled her close and kissed the top of her head. "I would do *anything* for you."

And he would still to this day.

Chris's thoughts returned to the present moment as they neared the south end of town and came to a little Lebanese café with the name Tabikh on a hand-painted sign. A poster in the window read "Grand Opening." He held the door for her, and she stepped inside. A savory aroma made his stomach growl. *Mmm, what is that? It smells delicious.*

A short, olive-skinned, balding man greeted them. "Welcome, friends."

Chris turned to look at the man as he came around the reception desk. "Thank you. We saw the sign in the window. How long have you been open?"

"We opened last week. My wife is the chef, and our daughter is the server. I'm Elias, the chief bottle washer."

Chris chuckled. "Nice to meet you, Elias. I'm Chris, and this is Amy. It smells amazing in here. What does 'Tabikh' mean?"

"It's *friend* in Arabic. We hope everyone who comes inside feels like our friend." He waved his hand around the café. "Sit anywhere you would like. My daughter will be with you shortly."

Amy gave Elias a big smile. "Thank you. We already feel like friends."

Chris led her to a table near the window so they could watch the activity on the street.

Soon a lovely girl with dark hair and dark almond-shaped eyes approached them. She was as young as they were. She welcomed them as she handed them menus. "Hello. I'm Isra. Can I get you something to drink?"

He already knew Amy's preference. "Sure. We'll both have Cokes. Thanks."

Amy opened her menu, bit her lip as she scanned it, then looked up at him. "I've never eaten Lebanese food before. What are you going to have?"

"I heard from a friend that shawarma is a great dish. I'm having that."

"That's what I'll have too."

Her excited chatter let him off the hook for making conversation as they waited for their meal. His palms felt sweaty, and his stomach was doing flip flops thinking about his plan. *I need to calm down, so she doesn't suspect anything.* He raked his hand through his thick blond hair, then rested it on his pocket. Taking a deep breath, he let it out slowly.

His friend was right—shawarma was a great dish. Isra explained it was a spiced mixture of many meats and cooked on a rotisserie. Chris enjoyed the tender, tasty slices of meat and the accompaniments of parsley salad, homemade bread, and especially the garlicky yogurt sauce and hummus. They both ate their fill, murmuring in appreciation.

When they left the restaurant, Amy tugged on his arm. "I *loved* that place. I hope someday we can go back there. The food was delicious, and Isra was so sweet."

He squeezed her hand. "Me too. Are you ready for the next adventure?" He was feeling more relaxed and looked forward to continuing their day.

"Sure, lead the way."

She looked up at him with a sweet, dimpled smile. He'd loved those dimples from that first moment they'd met in the college cafeteria when she'd come in with her friend Yolanda to sit with him and his roommate, Jon. And again—when he'd seen her at Jon's parents' lake house. It was a look he hoped to cherish the rest of his life.

Chris pulled her hand through the crook of his elbow as they walked through old neighborhoods, and he mentioned points of interest like a tour guide would. She oohed and aahed over every detail he had researched. After the tour, they returned to the car. He retrieved two bottles of cold water from the back hatch then jumped in the front seat and started the car.

He handed a bottle to her and took a gulp of his. "Are you tired yet? How about we go sit in the park before we leave for home?"

"That sounds perfect. I am tired, but I'm not ready to leave. A park sounds awesome." She sipped her water then leaned her head back. "I really appreciate all the homework you did for this date."

In a few minutes, he made his way to the Rochester Municipal Park. They got out of the car and walked hand in hand down a sidewalk past a pond. The sun was high in the sky, and he was sweaty. He casually brushed his hand across his pocket. His big moment was getting close.

He remembered the map he had studied and took a left next to a small creek meandering through the park.

Slowing his pace, he found a perfect bench facing a bend in the creek with bushes that shielded it from view. As they sat down on the shady bench, the water bubbled invitingly over the rocks in the creek.

She leaned into him, and he put his arm around her. "Ahh ... it's nice and cool here. The water sounds refreshing. I love everything about this town. The effort you made to arrange all this makes me feel special."

He thought again to that time at Jon's parents' lake house and how he and Amy had sat next to one another near a campfire. The night they'd shared their first kiss.

He pulled her closer to him now. "I was hoping you'd love it. I put this together because you *are* special."

He cupped her chin in his hand and kissed her. His lips were insistent, and passion awoke instantly. Before he lost control and strayed from his plan, he broke the kiss and slid to the ground at her feet. His hands reached for hers as he looked up at her surprised face.

"Chris ... what are you ...?" Her eyes filled with tears.

"Amy, this beautiful old town has a sense of permanence. That's why I wanted to bring you here today. We have been growing closer, and I want it to continue ... permanently." He paused and swallowed hard. "Amy Anderson, I want to enjoy a long, happy life together, and I am sure the best times are in front of us. It begins the moment you say yes!" He fumbled in his pocket for the tiny ring box. Opening it, he presented the ring to her with shaking hands. "Will you marry me?"

"Yes, oh yes!" she whispered between sobs of joy.

He reached for her hand and carefully fit the sparkling ring on her finger.

She swiped her tears away, then reached her arms out to hug him.

Scrambling up from his knees, he nearly fell over trying to hug her at the same time.

He got up on the bench next to her, encircling her with his arm. He pumped his fist high in the air and yelled, "We're getting married!"

They laughed and then kissed again, this time with the promise of a future together. She laid her head on his shoulder, holding her hand in front of her to admire the ring.

"It's gorgeous. I love it." She turned her head to look at him.

"Oh good. Yo helped me pick it out."

He sat with the girl of his dreams in his arms, watching the gurgling creek until they lost track of time. Finally, he glanced at his watch. It was getting late, and everyone would be waiting for them.

"I hate to end this part of our date. But there's more to come. Is it okay if we go now?"

"Of course. Although I can't imagine what could top this."

He grinned. "You'll have to wait and see."

She kept staring at her ring and beaming up at him as they walked, so he had to guide her to the car.

Amy had made him the happiest guy on the planet since that first meeting three years ago. And he knew she'd continue to make him happy for years to come. He was pumped and ready to let the party begin. *We're getting married!*

As they drove west, the warm sun shimmered on the hood of the shiny car, but Amy's eyes remained glued on her glittering ring as she held it out in front of her. A million thoughts ping-ponged through her mind. When would they set a date? What would her dress look like? Who would they ask to stand up for them at the wedding? She couldn't wait to tell everyone.

"One last stop before we reach your parents' house. Are you ready for dinner?"

"Of course. Oh, I can't *wait* to get home and tell everyone the news."

Chris exited the highway and turned right at the end of the ramp, then pulled up in front of a cobblestone restaurant. A pair of French doors stood open, inviting them in.

The hostess led them to a patio in the back of the restaurant. He moved aside and let Amy go out first.

As soon as she stepped down onto the slate floor, she heard, "Surprise!" She looked up to see the happy faces of their families and friends. Everyone was talking at once, hugs were plentiful, and laughter filled the air.

Amy's mom was first in line for an embrace, with her sister Ronnie close behind. Dad clapped Chris on the back and gave his daughter a squeeze. Her bestie Yo came next, along with Yo's boyfriend, Marcus.

Amy lifted her hand for her friend to see. "I love it! Thanks for helping Chris." Yo held her hand and inspected the beautiful ring.

Chris's best friend Jon peered around Marcus's broad shoulders. "Hey, when's it gonna be our turn?"

Marcus and Yo stepped out of the way, and Jon wrapped his arms around his buddy while his fiancée Jackie hugged Amy.

"I knew you could do it." Jon pulled back and punched Chris in the arm. Turning to Amy, he said, "From the moment Chris laid eyes on you, he was a goner. I was getting ready to wipe the drool off his chin in the school cafeteria that day you two met."

Amy giggled. "I'm just glad Chris didn't give up on me when I played hard to get."

Jon reached out to put his arm around Jackie. "Both Chris and I are marrying up."

More of their college friends and other family members crowded around to look at the ring on her finger and congratulate the couple. They all wanted to hear the engagement story, and Chris obliged them.

As her husband-to-be wove the story, Amy looked around at the people gathered. She noticed Chris's mom and his sister Carrie in the back of the crowd. They had come all the way from the Upper Peninsula of Michigan, but his dad was missing. Amy frowned, wondering why he wasn't there. She knew her parents wouldn't miss this for the world. How could Chris's dad have skipped such an important event, even if he had to drive seven hours one way from the U.P.? Despite his own marriage to Chris's mother being on the rocks, how could he do this to his son? She glanced at Chris. Had he noticed his dad was missing?

"... and she said yes!" Amy smiled at the cheers as Chris finished their engagement story.

The crowd dispersed a bit, and she turned to Chris and squeezed his hand. "I can't believe you surprised me again."

He leaned in for a kiss and then pulled her into the crowd. They began moving around to talk to the people in the back of the room. When they approached Chris's mom, she stood and reached her arms out to them. Amy noticed dark circles under her eyes and a drawn look to her face.

"Mom, where's Dad?"

So, he had noticed.

Mrs. McGrath began to tear up and glanced at Chris's sister. Amy noticed Carrie had tears in her eyes too. But not the happy tears her own mother'd had just moments earlier.

"Mom? What happened? Is Dad okay? Talk to me." Chris kept his voice low and motioned for his mom to sit. He and Amy sat down next to her.

"Honey, Dad is fine. He's okay. I'm so sorry to have to tell you this, today of all days." She took a deep breath and frowned. "He left. Yesterday. It's been a long time coming. It's finally over."

Her words hit Amy in the pit of her stomach. The stories Chris had told her of constant bickering and conflict were familiar to her. The never-ending struggle to make ends meet had caused his parents to work long hours, then retreat into separate rooms when they came home late. Amy felt bad for Chris not growing up in a stable family like she had. This was horrible news and the worst timing.

How would Chris take this? She looked up at the set face of her future husband—his jaw clenched, his eyes hard.

He stood and reached out to gather what was left of his family in his arms. "Mom, Carrie, whatever you need, I'm here for you. I can't believe his lousy timing, but I can't say it's a shock to me." They were all silent for a long moment.

Amy moved toward Chris, and he reached out to include her in the group hug.

"Mrs. McGrath, Carrie, I'm so sorry to hear this. Please let me know if there is anything I can do." She struggled to stay calm and not draw attention from the rest of the party.

The rest of the evening went by in a blur for Amy. Staying close to Chris, she tried to encourage him, but she knew he was hurting.

Her heart swelled with gratitude for the example of her parents. Remembering how they always took time for a weekly date night, she appreciated how they invested in keeping the flames alive. She hoped she would never forget her own parents' example. She was confident Chris's love for her was a forever kind of love as well. Would that be enough for them to thrive in their marriage?

After dinner, Chris and Amy stood in the parking lot waving goodbye to their guests. He saw Jon helping Jackie into their car. Chris wanted a moment alone with Jon, and he motioned his friend over.

Jon approached with a smile. "What a great party. We're so excited for you guys. Is your dad okay? I thought he would be here."

Chris shook his head and pressed his lips together. "I guess he's okay." He blurted out the painful words. "But my parents are getting a divorce. Dad's moved out, and Mom can't keep the house. I can't believe they couldn't have worked things out. I don't think they even considered the impact this will have on Carrie and me."

Jon stayed silent for a few beats before saying, "Wow. I can't even imagine. That's rough."

Chris raked his hands through his hair. "It's a mess. I figured it might eventually come to this, but not at my engagement party. Thank goodness Amy's parents have a great relationship. Getting to know them has given me a different perspective on what a family can be."

Jon reached out to squeeze Chris's shoulder and said, "I'm sorry, but I'm glad you told me. You can vent anytime. I'm here for you."

Chris replied, "I know that. Thanks, bro."

They were brothers—in celebration and in mourning.

Present day—March 19. Evening

Amy blew out a lingering sigh, trying to expel all her bottled-up frustration. She shifted in her seat and adjusted her seat belt, but she couldn't release the tension that had set up camp between her shoulders.

I can't change Chris's obstinance about his health. It's not my job. I'm not his mother. I've got to leave it alone. There are more important battles to win in our rocky marriage. She forced herself to unclench her hands from the steering wheel and focus on the task of finding a parking spot in the city at night. Thank goodness it wasn't snowing.

Circling the block in downtown Rochester, she looked for the best place to land for a parking-challenged woman. As she rounded the corner, she spotted a car leaving and was overjoyed to find two spots adjoining each other. Having the luxury of two spots to pull in and shift back and forth a few times was a good omen. Maybe tonight would bring her some relief—a happy distraction at her favorite café with her marriage mentor, Linda.

Fluffing up her straight, shoulder-length, auburn hair, she swung her long legs out of her Lexus RX. She looked up and saw Yolanda striding down the sidewalk toward her pottery studio. They waved and smiled at each other as they hurried to their separate destinations.

Gotta call Yo. She'll have some advice on the struggles Chris and I are having. Yo always tells me the truth—never pulls any punches. She's not exactly high on marriage after her divorce, but I know she'll have my best interests at heart.

Amy remembered the first time she'd met her college roommate when they'd almost run into each other outside the residence bathrooms. Yolanda's beautiful black face had been framed by long soft curls and a black headband like her own. She'd felt an instant connection with Yo's fun and vibrant attitude and had been overjoyed to find out they were roommates. Despite having totally different personalities—Yo's unorganized and carefree style clashed with her own organized and punctual one—they'd been friends ever since.

Pulling her soft gray scarf closer to her neck, she hurried through the frosty March air. She slipped into Tabikh, uncharacteristically late, despite having found such a gem of a parking spot. Months had passed since she had seen her mentor, months of dragging her feet before agreeing to a meeting.

The aroma of spiced meats rising from the grills at the back of the café enticed her. She took in the familiar room filled with laughter and banter, feeling as if she had come home. *This used to be my happy place. Why have I stayed away?* There in a booth by a window, Linda sat in a bright purple sweater, a white scarf wrapped around her neck, her silver hair styled fashionably. Amy hurried toward the booth.

Linda stood to wrap her in a warm embrace, then she stepped back. "I've missed you, girl."

"Same here. I'm glad we were finally able to get together. It's been too long. I'm sorry I didn't respond to your email last month ... things kind of got crazy." She busied herself with removing her scarf and coat while avoiding eye contact.

"No worries at all. I'm glad to see you. Have a seat, and let's order. I'm starving!"

Amy settled into her seat and picked up her menu, although she already knew what she wanted. The memory of tender, juicy shawarma with its distinctive warming spices made her mouth water.

Isra appeared at the table with a wide smile. "Greetings, Amy. I haven't seen you in forever. I've missed you and Chris."

"I've missed you too. And I've missed this amazing food. How's your dad doing? I saw him in the kitchen, working hard as usual." She forced herself to smile and make polite conversation even though her heart inside was breaking.

You're not the only one who misses Chris. I hate arguing in public so much I usually just stay home.

"Dad is doing well. He does work hard, but I don't think he would know what to do with himself if he didn't have his work. This café gives him purpose since Mama died." Isra took her pad out and jotted down their orders, then returned to the kitchen.

When their beverages arrived, Amy clinked glasses with Linda. "I haven't thanked you for being my marriage mentor. You have gone above and beyond in reaching out to me, then patiently waiting for me to get back to you. I keep wondering if you're going to give up on me." She took a tiny sip of her water, then bit the inside of her lip.

After taking her own sip, Linda put down her glass and clasped her hands together in front of her on the table. "It's my pleasure to be here for you. I do wonder sometimes if you're going to tell me you're done. But if you are still willing to meet and work on your marriage, I'm in."

"Thanks for your patience ... I sure need it." Amy tucked a bit of her hair behind her ear.

"Don't we all?"

At that moment, a little girl darted up to them, decked out in a red velvet dress, toy high heels, and bright red lipstick. She twirled and announced that she was a "pwincess." Linda grinned at her as a frazzled-looking young couple rushed up to the table. The young woman apologized, and the young man tried to grab the squirming youngster. The toddler was having none of their actions and squealed loudly, darting behind another table to escape capture.

Linda chuckled. "Do you remember your toddlers running around in restaurants? I want to say to the parents, 'Don't forget you two are on the same team. It *will* get better.'"

"Oh my, yes." Amy blew out a breath. "Brad and Michelle were a handful at times. There were a couple of years when we couldn't go out anywhere. The kids would throw tantrums, then Chris and I would start fighting too."

Linda nodded. "Before long you'll be grandparents like Jim and me. Then you'll have to calm down your kids when their babies give them headaches."

Amy shook her head, doubting if grandchildren would help her marriage. When she saw Linda waiting for her response, she said, "It's hard to believe Michelle and Brad are in college now but imagining them as parents ... I can't even go there." She took another sip from her glass. "I really miss them—they're so far away. But I am grateful Chris's mom and sister are only twenty minutes from them. His mom is the best grandma. We all adore her."

Linda took a sip of her drink. "Oh yes, I remember you said the kids are in the same area of the Upper Peninsula where Chris grew up."

"Yep. It's kind of ironic. Chris couldn't wait to leave the U.P. and pursue the financial success his parents never had. But the twins couldn't wait to go north and become Yoopers."

"Yoopers?" Linda cocked her head.

"Yes, that's the nickname for people from the U.P."

"Hey, before I forget to ask, we're still praying about Chris's headaches. What's the latest? Is he still having them?"

"Thanks. It's still an ongoing process. Tomorrow, he's got two more appointments. But I'm sure nothing will come of them." Amy sat forward and leaned her chin in her hand. "In his last physical, they found evidence of an irregular heartbeat. Since that can sometimes cause headaches, he went to a cardiologist for more bloodwork, an EKG, and a stress test. Tomorrow he will get the results of all that."

"What's the second appointment for?"

"Oh, that's an MRI on his brain, but it seems like a stab in the dark. Headaches are difficult to diagnose, and I wonder if they ran out of conditions to test for."

Their food arrived, and Isra gently set the plates in front of the women. "Is there anything else I can get you right now?"

Amy assured her they had everything they needed. She leaned forward and inhaled, remembering the first time she and Chris ate here the day he proposed. Savoring the memory of that happy day, she wondered when her joy had disappeared. Her heart ached as she scooped up a large portion of shawarma and blew the steam away. While it was cooling, she looked at Linda. "I heard you recently celebrated your anniversary."

Linda beamed. "Yes, can you believe it? Forty-three years. Seems so incredible to me. To celebrate, we took a short trip to Mexico and lounged on the beach. It was wonderful."

"Wow, forty-three years? That's amazing! It seems like an impossible dream for us." Amy put her fork down and tried to sound happy for her marriage mentor. "I admire you and Jim. He seems totally devoted to you, and he loves God. You have the perfect marriage."

Linda laughed out loud. "There *are* no perfect marriages. We do get along most days now, but it wasn't always that way. We had a lot of struggles for many years of our marriage." She paused, setting her fork down. "There was a time when I wasn't confident we would make it to twenty-five years, let alone forty-three."

"Seriously? I never would have guessed. What happened?"

Linda pursed her lips. "It's hard to put a finger on when it all started. I think these things kind of creep up on you. We had normal problems. Not so different from the couple with the energetic toddler. But we didn't work together as a team. We let the problems divide us, and we each blamed the other."

"What kinds of things, if you don't mind me asking?" Amy's meal remained untouched.

"We had kids early in our marriage. It was challenging since we were so young. We were barely grown up ourselves, and now we had children to raise. Meanwhile, Jim was advancing in his career, working long hours, and traveling a lot. I was a stay-at-home mom without a husband around—I was resentful and exhausted."

Amy groaned. "Not only did I have twins, but I've *worked* their whole lives, so I can understand feeling resentful and exhausted. Did you have anyone you could talk to, like a marriage mentor?" She finally took a bite of her meal.

"Nope. We had no one to talk to, other than friends who were as clueless as we were. At least not right away. Marriage mentoring wasn't something we had ever heard of." Linda shook her head. "I was sure the problem was all on his end, and I tried to convince him we should see a marriage counselor. But you can guess how well that went." She rolled her eyes.

Amy's heart sank. Was everyone's marriage a mess?

Linda waved her fork. "But our story has a happy ending. Many real-life stories do. I'll tell you about it *only* after we enjoy our meals. Yours has barely been touched."

"Deal." Amy smiled, warmed by Linda's promise of hope. Her mood lightened as they chitchatted over their delicious dinners.

Suddenly, a piercing wail startled Amy, and she put down her fork. She turned around to look. The red-gowned cherub's sippy cup had opened, and milk had spilled all over her beautiful dress. The young mother mopped up the spill with Isra's help, but the child was inconsolable. All eyes were on their table. Amy watched in dismay as the young man shoved his phone in his pocket and glared at the woman. Then he stood, turned on his heels, and stomped out of the restaurant. The young woman paid the bill, collected her miserable ragamuffin, and scurried out of the café with her head down.

Amy felt the woman's embarrassment. "Isn't that just like a man?" she said to Linda. "The poor woman has no one to help her. It's unbelievable he got up and walked out on her. Just last week, Chris walked out on me when we were having pizza."

Linda's soft voice did not mimic Amy's hard one. "I remember difficult times like that ... but like I said, things improved for us."

After Isra delivered a plate of baklava to share between them, Amy leaned in toward her mentor. "So, what happened to change your marriage?"

Linda finished chewing a sticky bite of pastry, then said, "It all started with my neighbor, Joan. One day, I broke down and cried on her shoulder. I was at my wit's end. I had constant thoughts about leaving Jim, but it was too overwhelming to figure out how to make it alone. I was stuck." Linda pushed another bit of her pastry onto her fork but didn't take the bite. "It felt good to let go and share what was bothering me. Joan hugged me, handed me a tissue, and told me I needed a supportive community. She invited me to come to her church, and I went the same week. It was the beginning of a new life for me, a new life for Jim, and a new life for our marriage. We've never looked back."

Amy's body went rigid as she listened to Linda's story. She felt her face flush. "We've been Christians for years. I've been in Bible studies, volunteered in women's ministry, even memorized verses. What more do I need to do? Church hasn't helped." She put her piece of baklava down and looked directly at Linda. "Nothing I've done has changed Chris. I had such high hopes for us when we got serious about God and renewed our vows. But things are just getting worse. That's why I haven't responded to your emails. I don't think mentoring is working. Chris is as remote as ever. My love for him is running cold. I don't know if it will ever come back." Tears welled up in her eyes, and a sob escaped her lips.

Linda reached out and put her hand on Amy's arm. "Thank you for being so honest with me. I do understand."

Amy used her napkin to blot her tears as Linda continued.

"For me, it wasn't about what I needed to *do*. I had to learn who God created me to *be*. He didn't intend for me to be a control freak. I had a choice as I grieved crushing disappointments. I could respond by trusting God and building my faith or rejecting God and destroying it. Gradually, I embraced who I am and who God is. I responded with peace and confidence when things went wrong. Jim noticed the change in me and wanted what I had." She paused a moment. "Does that make sense?"

Amy pushed the last piece of baklava around on her plate. She wanted to believe Linda. But it sounded too pat, too simplistic. She *had* changed, but Chris hadn't changed at all. He wasn't even going to church with her anymore. *I'm afraid I don't have what it takes to trust God the way Linda does.* She pushed the thoughts away, determined not to cry anymore. Looking up at Linda, she pressed her lips together.

"What a great story. I'm so happy for you. Thanks for sharing with me." Amy suddenly felt the need to get away, to remove herself from this moment. She glanced at her watch. "It's been great catching up with you, but I need to run now."

Linda picked up her purse from the seat beside her, then reached for the bill. "I'm sorry, I didn't realize it was getting so late. I'll get this. Feel free to call me anytime. I am here for you."

They rose from the table and hugged before Amy slipped on her coat and shouldered her way out the door into the chill night.

March 19. Night

Linda hurried to her car around the corner from the café, cinching her scarf tighter against the frigid wind. The engine roared to life, and the heater resumed its windstorm from the trip into town. As she guided her car toward home, she rehearsed her conversation with Amy. *I don't know if I handled that right. She finally opened to me, but after I shared my experience, it seemed like the door slammed shut. Was my story too challenging for her to hear?*

As she entered the house, she peeled off her coat and scarf, rubbed her hands together, and headed into the family room. Jim sat on the sofa in front of the fireplace. She joined him, swinging her legs up under a throw and tucking its warmth around her. They kissed, and she leaned her head on his shoulder. He wrapped his hands around hers to warm them.

He had muted the TV, but she noticed masked and gowned medical workers pushing a patient on a stretcher into an ambulance while other people held sheets up to shield the patient from the cameras. "What's going on? Is this a movie?"

"No, it's the news." He scratched his chin with his hand. "Do you remember hearing about a virus outbreak in China? Looks like it's arrived in the States. This is a nursing home in the state of Washington where many patients have been infected." Jim unmuted the TV so they could hear the story.

She was surprised seventy-four people in Washington had already died, and almost fourteen hundred cases of this mysterious virus had been identified. But it seemed too far away to be a threat to them.

They continued watching the news, but she had trouble paying attention. Her eyelids grew heavy, and she yawned. "I'm about done in tonight, and too disappointed by my conversation with Amy to listen to more bad news."

Jim turned off the TV and put his hands in hers. "We got sidetracked by the news story. What happened with Amy?"

She sighed. "I don't know how to help her. When I contact her, it takes weeks before she responds to me. Then I try to encourage her, but she doesn't seem willing to believe that her marriage *can* improve. It seems like she has a lot of negative feelings about Chris always just beneath the surface, waiting to erupt. For instance, we saw a man walk out on a woman in the restaurant tonight after a struggle with their toddler. Amy responded with, 'Isn't that just like a man,' then jumped in with a story about how Chris walked out on her in a pizza restaurant."

Jim raised his eyebrow and said, "I've heard a little more of that pizza date episode. Chris used that night to illustrate how he thinks Amy is out to control him, especially about his food choices."

"How so?" Linda asked.

"Well, according to Chris, Amy wanted a veggie pizza and Chris wanted the meat lover's pizza. Of course, Chris didn't tell me he walked out on her, just like Amy didn't offer up how the fight started."

Linda shook her head in frustration. "There're always two sides to every story." She rubbed her neck. "I'm afraid my attempts to challenge her tend to result in her avoiding me. Tonight, she said she doesn't think Chris will ever change and that her love for him has run cold. In her view, mentoring isn't working. But I think she's stuck in old habits and doesn't realize it. She must make changes too—if their marriage is to succeed."

She placed her head on his shoulder and continued, "They both captured my heart the same way all our couples have. I dream for their marriage to thrive, but it's frustrating when I can see the solution, yet I have to sit and wait for God to work."

"I know exactly what you mean. But our role isn't to fix them. We can point them in the right direction, but they must take the next steps."

She blew out a breath. "I know. But patience isn't my strong suit. I want to see *results*."

He looked up and steepled his fingers in front of his mouth. "Only God knows what's going on beneath the surface. Do you remember the story of how the Chinese bamboo trees grow? After planting the seeds, it takes a full five years before anything is seen above ground. During that time, only the root structure is growing. Anyone who doesn't understand the Chinese bamboo might quit watering and give up hope before the fifth year. But something is happening beneath the surface, and once the sprouts start to appear above ground, they can grow up to ninety feet in just five weeks."

Linda nodded as she remembered the story. "Yes, I do remember that. How incredible. Do you think Chris and Amy are like Chinese bamboo trees?"

"Without a doubt. It's been years—I think eight—since they joined the church. They told us they had made a commitment to be all in for God and renewed their vows. But their growth has been in fits and starts. We've met with them for ... how many years now, maybe three? And we haven't seen much change in them. They're both blaming each other for everything. I've been doing that Bible study with Chris, which has been challenging. He seems to understand, but I don't know if his heart is changing. He doesn't share much of a personal nature. He still wants to keep a secret from Amy that he's doing the study with me. And there's no progression in their marriage."

Linda nodded thoughtfully.

Jim leaned in. "So ... we can't stop watering now. God is still engineering a powerful root structure in their lives. Don't give up hope. They are going to make it, and when they do, it's going to be amazing. They need our grace and prayers to nurture their budding hearts more than ever. As they are ready for it, we can challenge them with biblical truth. One day, before you know it, we'll see the green shoots poking up from the ground. These two are destined for something great together."

"Yes, I agree." Linda smiled and savored the hope filling her.

Jim stood, pulling her with him. "How about we get ready for bed? It's been a long day."

She nodded through a huge yawn as he helped her off the sofa and followed her into the bedroom.

Jim waited for her to finish her nightly routine and slip into bed. She snuggled under the covers and scooted over so he could spoon her. Encircling her with his arm, he held her close until he felt her relax in his arms.

After a few minutes, he heard her bedtime mantra. "I'm so glad I get to sleep next to you."

"I'm so glad I get to sleep next to you too, hon."

In no time at all, he heard her soft, regular breathing.

He gently unwound himself and rolled over, leaving his sleeping wife to her dreams. It was just like her to share frustration about something late in the evening and then nod off to sleep, leaving him wide awake trying to figure out how to address the matter.

She gets problems off her mind by giving them to me. I should remember that's not my monkey. I need to let the monkey go and instead be an empathetic listener.

He waited a few minutes, eyes closed, breathing deeply and slowly. But it wasn't working. The monkey was doing somersaults in his head. *Is the monkey staying in my mind because I haven't turned the corner with Chris either?*

Thinking back to other couples they had mentored, he realized that usually the husband was the first to give up working on the marriage. *I'm glad Chris hasn't quit. It's a good sign that he's sticking with our Bible study.*

Lord, please give Linda the patience and perseverance to continue with Amy. Please give me the right approach with Chris to lead him in this Bible study. We know we cannot invest more in their marriage than they do, so we ask you to step in as needed, especially when we are out of ideas.

This time, the monkey fell asleep too.

When Love Promised— Twenty-Eight Years Ago

Amy turned around to look over her shoulder in the mirror. She wanted to see every angle of her wedding dress. "I love it. It's exactly what I had in mind, Mom." She admired the elegant V back of her dress in the mirror as she clasped a slim belt around her waist and adjusted the simple jeweled headband around her permed auburn hair.

Then, she followed her three attendants—Yolanda, Ronnie, and Carrie—and her mother to the back of the church where they waited for the signal to move down the aisle. Her father waited there for her.

"Let's get this party started." Amy took her dad's arm. He smiled down at her and patted her hand with his own.

Just then, she saw Chris's dad rush into the church with a younger woman on his arm. He nodded curtly to her, and they sat in the back row.

She sighed. *I hope Chris didn't notice him coming in so late with an unexpected guest. What a disappointment.*

Her dad turned to her and brushed a tendril of her hair aside. "You look beautiful. This is your day, Daughter. A day to celebrate all you and Chris have accomplished. You both have a wonderful future ahead of you. I'm proud of you." He leaned over and kissed her cheek.

"Thanks, Dad. This is a dream come true. Thank you for everything, especially for making Chris feel so welcomed in our family. I love you." She hugged him.

"I love you too, Sunshine. You know no one is ever going to be perfect enough for my daughter, but I love Chris like my own son. He did save you from drowning, after all."

She didn't have time to react as the first strains of "The Wedding March" began. Her stomach fluttered as she took the first steps toward the man of her dreams.

Pastor Mark stood at the center of the platform in her childhood church. Her family hadn't attended often in recent years, but she'd wanted to get married here. She had just met the new, young pastor a few months ago when they visited the church to talk about the wedding and had appreciated his good sense of humor. She looked to her right and left now and noticed friends and family standing and smiling as she passed them.

When she saw her soon-to-be husband next to Pastor Mark, the people and the pews disappeared, and Chris was the only one with her in the church. He bounced a little on his toes, wiping his hands on his pants. She smiled, glad he felt just as nervous as she did on this momentous day.

At the front of the church, she stopped with her dad. Chris shook hands with him. Then Dad kissed her and moved to sit down with Mom. She took Chris's arm and felt like she was home.

The pastor motioned for Chris's friend, Jon, to come forward and share the Scripture reading from Ecclesiastes 4:9–12. "Two are better than one, because they have a good return for their labor: if either of them falls down, one can help the other up. But pity anyone who falls and has no one to help them up. Also, if two lie down together, they will keep warm. But how can one keep warm alone? Though one may be overpowered, two can defend themselves. A cord of three strands is not quickly broken."

As Jon took his seat, the pastor turned to the congregation and said, "Chris and Amy will now share their vows they have written specifically for one another." Chris squeezed her hand, then let go to pull a rumpled bit of paper from his jacket pocket. He smoothed the paper a bit and began to read.

"I, Christopher James McGrath, take you, Amy Susan Anderson, to be my wedded wife. I promise to be your guiding light in the darkness, a warming comfort in the cold, and a shoulder to lean on when life is too much to bear alone. I promise to be there for better, for worse, for richer, for poorer, in sickness, and in health, to love and to cherish, till death do us part. Forsaking all others, I promise to love you as long as we both shall live."

Amy had memorized her vows, but now wished she had brought a three by five card. She cleared her throat and began.

"I, Amy Susan Anderson, take you, Christopher James McGrath, to be my wedded husband. I will always be your biggest fan, your constant supporter, and your best friend. I promise to be there for better, for worse, for richer, for poorer, in sickness, and in health, to love and to cherish, till death do us part. Forsaking all others, I promise to love you as long as we both shall live."

Amy followed Pastor Mark's instructions and the rest of the service went by in a blur. She could only focus on Chris's warm brown eyes. Abruptly, the ceremony was over, and she was walking down the aisle as Mrs. Christopher McGrath. Passing all their cheering family and friends, she felt a thrill rush through her. She'd never been so happy in her life.

Chris set the heavy luggage down in front of a ticket machine and punched in the destination. He looked over at Amy who was struggling to keep her eyes open after flying to Munich for their honeymoon. The machine spit out their tickets.

"Hang in there, wife. We'll be at our hotel in no time."

She yawned. "Wow, am I glad you know how to navigate train stations in Germany. I would be lost without you."

"We board at the platform over there." He pointed to the right and picked up the luggage. "We'll have to hustle because it boards in a few minutes. They don't wait for stragglers."

Their forty-minute trip to the old town was quiet. He wanted to sleep, but he didn't dare close his eyes for fear of missing the announcement for their stop. He had to pay close attention to catch the names rattled off in German. Amy, on the other hand, snoozed on his shoulder. When he heard their stop announced, he put his hand on her knee. "Wake up, beautiful. We're here."

The train pulled away, leaving them standing on the platform. He felt like he had been run over by a bus. Amy's stylish pantsuit was wrinkled, but her smile was bright as she looked around.

When they reached their hotel and checked into their room, they both fell on the puffy white duvet and sighed loudly. Amy yawned. "I'm so tired. That was the longest flight ever."

"It was. I'm exhausted too." He couldn't help yawning in response. "Let's take a nap before we walk around the old city."

She snuggled next to him. "Mm ... sounds good."

He caressed her hair. "I can't wait to show you some of the things I experienced when I was at Technical University Munich for my fellowship. Taking advanced robotics courses and helping a PhD student gather data for his dissertation was thrilling, but it was lonely being away from you. Each time I saw something new, I imagined how much better it could have been with you by my side. Can you believe the day has finally come?"

She kissed him. "Babe, we're so fortunate to have found one another. I'm totally in love with you. Everything is turning out perfectly for us. And you arranged this amazing honeymoon. What a great way to start our lives as husband and wife."

After a short nap, they sat at an outdoor café with pastries and coffee in the famous Marienplatz square.

Chris pointed. "That column is the Mariensäule. The gold statue on the top represents the Virgin Mary."

"Wow, that's beautiful." She pulled out her camera. "How old is it?"

"Well, this square goes back to the twelfth century when it was the market square where everyone met to buy and sell goods. The Mariensäule wasn't added until 1638. It was erected to show gratitude to the Swedes for not destroying Munich during the Thirty Years' War. This became known as Marienplatz, which means Mary's square."

It was obvious to him that she loved the sights and sounds as much as he did. The ancient buildings held secrets and stories. There was nothing like this in the States. That's why he wanted to come back and share it with her.

She finished the last bite of pastry and washed it down with more of the rich coffee. "Just what I needed. Coffee and pastry are the perfect combination to help me stay awake today."

He lifted his cup and inhaled. "I've missed this strong coffee. The Germans think our coffee is just brown water. You'll probably need several cups of coffee as the day goes by. Getting over jet lag takes a while."

"No kidding. It feels like I didn't sleep at all on the plane. I kept thinking about our wedding." She yawned. "It was magical."

"Yeah. It was. I couldn't believe I was marrying the most gorgeous woman in the world."

He saw a pink blush rise in her cheeks. "And I was marrying the prince of my dreams." She leaned her chin in her hands and looked at him. "Everything was absolutely *perfect*."

He took some pastry crumbs and tossed them to the birds nearby as a feeling of sadness dampened his joy. "*Almost* perfect." He looked back up at her. "I can't help feeling angry with my dad. Can you believe he showed up with another woman?"

Amy reached over and grabbed his hand. "I know. I was hoping you didn't notice right before the wedding started. I'm sad about your parents' divorce. I wish I could help you feel better, but I don't know how."

He squeezed her hand. "Knowing I have you to confide in makes me feel better. My parents will do whatever they want. Nothing anyone can do about that." He pulled his hand away and rubbed his jaw. "The way I see it, their divorce didn't solve any problems. It just created more."

She nodded.

He tilted his head and looked at her. "You know, there is something you can do. Will you make a pact with me? Let's promise we will never consider divorce as a solution to problems."

"That's an awesome idea." She placed her right hand over her heart and took a deep breath. "I, Amy McGrath, hereby promise I will never consider divorce as a solution for whatever problems we may have. So help me God."

He followed suit, placing his right hand over his heart. She came over to his seat and sat on his lap. They sealed their oaths with a lingering kiss.

March 19. Late Night

Chris stepped out of the shower and toweled dry. Then he changed the sheets on the bed thinking his preparations might relax his wife enough to lead to some cuddle time. He missed the spontaneity of their early marriage and hoped his thoughtfulness would be just the thing she needed. Amy had been out of sorts lately. He wasn't sure exactly why, but he felt he must be responsible. Climbing into bed, he tried to stay awake. There was an old sitcom on the TV, but he wasn't really interested.

Finally, he heard the back door slam downstairs and moments later, the creaking of the steps as Amy came upstairs. Quickly reaching over, he switched on the heated mattress pad on her side of the bed. Rolling over to face the bedroom door, he propped himself up on his elbow.

When he saw her face, his hopes faded a little. A scowl creased her forehead.

He decided to press forward and maybe charm her out of her mood. "Hey, babe, I'm glad you're home. I warmed up your side of the bed for you." He raised his eyebrows and gave her his best smile.

Amy barely glanced at him. "Hmm. I'm exhausted."

"Did your meeting with Linda go okay?"

"Not really. I don't know why I keep meeting with her. I don't get much out of it." Amy passed by him on her way to the bathroom.

Waiting for her to return, he racked his brain trying to decide what to say next.

She came out of the bathroom and got her slippers out of the closet, then pulled on her robe.

He sat up in bed, swinging his legs over the edge. "Where are you going? Aren't you tired?"

"I'm going to sleep in the spare room tonight. I was up most of last night because of your snoring. If you won't get tested for sleep apnea, I don't know why I keep sleeping in here."

Not this again. His stomach clenched. He spoke slowly and firmly. "We both know that sleep apnea makes people tired during the day, and I'm never tired. I have lots of energy. I think you are a light sleeper."

Her face tightened. "I was never a light sleeper before I married you. It must be nice not to be tired. I'm exhausted after trying to sleep with a congested rhino."

"Even if I do have sleep apnea, we both know half the people who try a CPAP machine eventually give up. That's not a ringing endorsement for a horrible contraption. Who wants to wear that awful headgear? No thanks. I don't have sleep apnea, and that's the end of the story." He folded his arms.

"Go ahead and keep thinking that. We're spending hundreds of dollars for all the meaningless tests you're having for the headaches. Nothing, I mean not one single test, has revealed anything at all." He heard her voice getting louder and faster. "It's unbelievable that you won't get this test for your health, for me, for our marriage. I'm just trying to help you be better. Isn't that what wives are for? Why are you so sensitive? We can't even talk about this without a fight." She turned and stomped out of the bedroom. A second later, he heard the spare bedroom door slam.

Chris punched his pillow. She was right about one thing. They couldn't talk about this without a fight. This argument was like many others that had become well-practiced dance routines, which they repeated often. His blood would start boiling as soon as she headed down one of those familiar paths. It always ended with one of them stuffing it and walking away. If he felt responsible, he would come home with flowers the next day. Then they would pretend nothing happened. Rinse, repeat.

He got up and went to the bathroom to splash cold water on his red face. All his good intentions were washed away and replaced by a pounding headache.

When Love Blossomed— Twenty-Three Years Ago

Amy wiped her brow with the back of her hand as she surveyed the mess of boxes strewn over the tiny kitchen floor. *This is so exciting. I can't wait to cook my first dinner in our first home.*

She watched Chris across the kitchen from her. He stood on a stepladder, putting seldom-used items into the cupboard above the refrigerator. "Are you ready for a break? I'm getting hungry."

He grinned over his shoulder at her, stepped down, and took her in his arms. "I sure am. This is the last of the kitchen items. I'll break down these boxes before we leave. Should we walk to town for some lunch?"

"Sounds great. Then we can start painting the living room when we get back. I'm going to freshen up." She headed toward the bathroom, appreciating the homey squeaks from the old oak floors. She loved that sound. It reminded her of her grandmother's house.

She considered their house a find. They'd spent months waiting for the right historic house to come on the market in Rochester. It finally did, and she was thrilled when their offer was accepted. It was a Sears kit house built in 1923. She loved the large front porch and the small, fenced yard. The Craftsman-style bungalow was a little bit worn around the edges, making it feel like home the moment they moved in. The neighbors were friendly. She thought it would be the perfect place to raise kids.

She held his hand as they walked down their street and into the park. Taking this way was a little longer, but she loved walking past "their bench" where he proposed.

"We live in a magical place. Do you realize that?" She watched a duck cross the path in front of them. "I couldn't be happier. I was thinking how wise you were to make sure we had time to focus on each other before we took on the stress of home ownership. And I love that we're building a rainy-day fund for unexpected things. We've already made great progress on that."

"Thanks." He squeezed her hand. "I think my parents started off on the wrong foot financially. That led to working long hours apart and putting their relationship on the back burner." He stopped walking and pulled Amy close. "I want to do things differently."

She nodded. "I know. So do I."

He gave her a quick peck on the lips, then they continued walking hand in hand for several moments. "By the way," she said, "we need to decide about your job offer to join the new robotics firm as VP of Sales. Have you thought any more about it?"

"I can't stop thinking about it. It sounds too good to be true. A new, fully funded joint venture with mostly young staff. Not only is it a great opportunity, but I'd have stock options as well." He pressed his lips together.

"So, what's making you hesitate? I think it's a big break for you."

"A start-up requires a huge time commitment. I'm worried it'll be hard on us. Long hours and travel later. Are you ready for me to be working long hours? It'll put a lot on you to keep up with everything here. Will we be able to keep our relationship number one?"

She nodded. "Yes. I want you to have this opportunity. If that's the only reason you're holding back, don't. I'm willing to do more around the house to cover for you. I love you so much, and I know you have the skills and the vision to help build something great in this company. Please don't say no because of me."

He stopped and pulled her close once more, lifting her up off her feet and twirling her around. "Really? You mean it? Thank you! I hated to ask you to make sacrifices for my career, but I've been itching for an opportunity like this. I believe it's a once-in-a-lifetime break."

Joy filled her heart as he put her down, and they continued their walk to town.

She pointed across the street at an iconic burger joint. "Let's see if we can get seats at Red Knapp's Dairy Bar. I've been wanting to try it."

"Anything for my wife." He put his arm around her as they crossed the street.

They sat at the counter. She ordered a chocolate malt, and he ordered a Boston Cooler with their burgers. He told her a Boston Cooler was Detroit's own Vernors Ginger Ale with a scoop of ice cream floating in it, which sounded odd to her. She amused herself with twirling around on the red leather barstools and reading the old-fashioned product ads that lined the walls. She moaned a bit with the first bite of her delicious burger.

Chris's eyes widened, and he nodded. "Good call."

They both happily devoured their meals and shared their drinks. She liked the Boston Cooler.

She rubbed her stomach when they finished. "Whew, that was filling. But delicious."

He chuckled. "Don't worry. You'll burn it off with all the work we have to do."

"I love decorating, so this part will be fun." She hopped off the barstool.

"Race you home?" He lifted his eyebrows.

She punched him in the arm. "Carry me home?"

They bantered back and forth on the walk back.

When they returned, they changed into old clothes. She gathered the paint, brushes, and rollers while Chris covered the living room floor with a drop cloth.

She pulled out the record player, and they sang to classic rock as they painted. The windows were open, and a cool breeze blew in.

"Hey, Amy ... look." She turned around to see an impish smile on his face. His brush was pointing to a large heart painted on the wall behind him. Inside the heart it said "C + A ever."

She sauntered over to him, paintbrush in hand, and spoke in a fake southern drawl. "Mr. McGrath, that's a mighty fine work of art you created. But you left out the 'for' in 'forever.'"

He slipped into Yooper jargon. "No, ma'am. I didn't forget it. C is da turd letter and A is da furst. C plus A equals four, don't ya know? Four ... ever, eh." He removed his imaginary hat and bowed.

She took her wet brush and lightly tapped his muscled arm. "Is that so?"

He paused as his eyes locked on hers, then traced a long thin line of paint down her arm, finishing with a flourish.

She looked down at her arm, tossing her brush on the drop cloth that covered the floor. She took his face in her hands and kissed him, long and slow.

He dropped his brush and wrapped his arms around her.

She pulled away briefly to whisper, "We can finish painting tomorrow."

March 20. Morning

Chris awoke with a pounding headache. For the umpteenth time, he wrestled with the familiar feeling that something sinister was growing inside his skull. *What if it's a tumor? It's getting worse each day. What if I can't work anymore? Or worse?*

He slowly rolled out of bed and dragged himself to the bathroom. Blinking, he felt a stabbing pain when he looked at the light seeping in past the window blinds. He poured some water in a cup and swallowed a couple of pain killers. Then he rinsed a cloth with cold water and wrung it out. Returning to bed, he placed the damp cloth on his head and waited for relief. He felt nauseated.

He must have fallen asleep again, because the next thing he knew, Amy was shaking his arm.

"Chris, wake up. You're going to be late for your cardiologist appointment."

Opening one of his eyes a crack, he saw her standing by the side of the bed in her robe. He groaned in pain.

"My head feels awful today. I don't think I can drive. Should I change my appointment?"

Amy shook her head. "No, I'll take you. Maybe they'll have some new feedback from all your tests. And the doctor might be able to prescribe a stronger pain relief medicine."

Sitting up, he went through the motions to throw on some clothes and prepare to leave. As he moved around, he felt a little better. But the intense pain and sensitivity to light was new. *What's wrong with me? I've never felt nauseated before either. This is no run-of-the-mill headache. That's why all the tests have been negative. They haven't tested for a brain tumor. At least today, I'll have the MRI. Will today be the day the worst-case scenario I've imagined comes true?*

Chris was surprised when the sign posted on the cardiologist's door said only patients were allowed in the building because of the pandemic. Amy insisted on coming into the waiting room anyway. He knew she would be in a huff if she wasn't allowed in, so he tried to negotiate with the young woman behind the desk. "But there haven't been any deaths in our state and the governor hasn't issued any specific restrictions."

The assistant firmly stated it was "office policy," so Amy stomped off to the car.

The doctor's waiting room was empty, and Chris had no trouble finding a seat. What would the results show? Did he have a serious heart problem? He blew out a long breath. Finally, the nurse called him into the doctor's office.

The doctor told Chris he had a mild heart irregularity, but it wasn't serious. The doctor doubted Chris's headaches were related.

"Another dead end," Chris told Amy in the car a few minutes later.

Amy remained quiet, and he wondered what he might have done to upset her again.

"What's the matter? Still mad over last night?"

Flinging up her hands, she said, "Yes, I'm mad. I'm frustrated. How many more tests are they going to put you through before you agree to at least consider sleep apnea?"

Chris knew better than to keep the conversation going. "I don't know. Maybe we'll learn more at the MRI today." *Only a few more hours, and I'll know if it's a brain tumor.* He gritted his teeth as they drove home in stony silence.

March 20. Late Afternoon

After the appointment with the cardiologist, Chris spent the rest of the day working from his home office. He enjoyed the perks of management, especially the flexibility that came with his position. Amy stayed out of his way, but he assumed she was still sulking over the sleep apnea argument. *I'm only too happy to enjoy the silence.* When it was time to head to the MRI appointment, he powered down his computer and packed up his briefcase.

He stepped out of the house and admired the sapphire sky. Inhaling a deep breath, he relished the transition from the contentious atmosphere inside the house to the fresh air outside. The saying was a Michigan March comes in like a lion and goes out like a lamb. That was also true this very day. This morning, there had been sleet. Now the air was still cold, but there was no more sleet in the forecast, and the sun had melted the thin layer of ice on the pavement. He decided Jezebel, his Dodge Challenger Hellcat, could escape the prison of the garage where she sat brooding most of the winter. Shunning the practical-yet-boring SUV they had taken to this morning's appointment, he stepped around Amy's Lexus and stopped briefly to admire Jezebel. At least he would arrive in style for his dreaded MRI appointment.

Jezebel growled to life as he pressed the ignition button. He could feel the car's desire to lurch forward out of the garage. "Steady, girl. Gotta let the fluids circulate before I tap into all that horsepower." He looked up at the mirror and grinned at himself as he stepped on the gas and felt the rumble in his chest.

Ahhh. This is pure joy. And I sure need some joy right now. In no time I'll be stuffed into that MRI tube. I hope I can hold it together in there.

As he slowed to guide Jezebel into the imaging center parking lot, he looked up at the mirror again, only this time he grimaced. *Oh well, here I go, ready or not.* Parking the car, he retrieved the mask they gave him this morning at the doctor's office. Hooking it obediently around his ears, he extracted himself from the low-slung car and shuffled into the building. A masked and gloved attendant stopped him and asked several questions about his health, took his temperature, squirted hand sanitizer into his palm, and gave him a "well visitor" sticker. He could feel his face flush and his headache worsen as he headed for the radiology department.

After signing in, the receptionist led him to a dressing room and directed him to remove all his clothes and jewelry, then to put on a hospital gown and sit in the waiting room. There was only one other man in the waiting room, who looked equally apprehensive. Chris tried to catch his eye to say something witty, but the man kept his eyes averted. Chris took a seat, already feeling a bit claustrophobic because of the mask. *I hope they let me take the mask off in the tube.* He wiped his clammy hands on the gown and restlessly crossed and uncrossed his legs as he waited.

Anti-anxiety meds would have been a good idea. Too late now. I'll just have to bear it. Thinking about Jezebel parked outside waiting to whisk him to freedom gave him a little relief. Finally, a radiology tech came to usher him into the MRI room.

"I'm Geoff, and I'll be operating the MRI for you. You can hand me your mask, and I'll give it back after the test. I will be able to hear you during the test, so if you have any questions or concerns at any time just let me know. The sound is louder than a rock concert. Sort of the level of a construction jackhammer. You can either wear earplugs, or I can give you earphones and music to muffle the noise."

"If you have some jazz music, I'll take the earphones."

"Coming right up."

Chris positioned himself on the unyielding metal bed and tried to adjust his neck in the rigid head cradle.

Geoff handed him earphones. "The cradle is to ensure you hold your head perfectly still so we can get the best images."

Chris did his best to find a comfortable position as Geoff fitted a cage over his head and asked him if he was comfortable. When he said yes, Geoff said, "I'll be in the other room, and I'll talk to you through the headphones. Remember, I can hear you." He placed a button in Chris's hand. "You can squeeze this if you need to stop at any point, okay? But try to hold on and it'll go faster."

Soon the bed whirred as it slid into the tube. Chris kept his eyes shut so he wouldn't see the top of the tube several inches above him. Even so, he still imagined his middle-aged spread almost touching the top of the tunnel.

A few moments later, Geoff spoke into his earphones. "Is the music volume okay?"

"Yes, thanks."

"Good. Just try to relax. Let me know if you need anything. I'll be here the whole time."

A heavy banging alerted him the MRI had begun.

The strong beat of the jazz helped Chris stay calm but didn't drown out the noise. The metal table was hard and cold, and he tensed, trying not to move. It wasn't long before an ache began in the small of his back. He needed to focus on something else. Jim told him how important it was to be still and listen to God. Well, he had to be still right now, so this might be a good time. And that might take his mind off his suffocating claustrophobia.

God, I don't really want to dig up stuff, but I'll try. Please help me figure out what you want me to know.

As Chris let his mind wander, he recalled a time at church when the pastor had told a joke about work, religion, and play. "Some men are religious about work, they play at religion, and it is work for them to play." Amy had jabbed her elbow into his ribs, and he had glowered at her. There was some truth to what the pastor had said, although he wouldn't have admitted it at the time.

God, were you using Amy to get my attention? I ignored her jab and got mad at her instead. I can admit it now—I had my priorities wrong. I did play at religion and was religious about work. Way back in college, Jon tried to get me to join in the Christian fellowship. But I didn't think I needed that. I had my life all figured out. We got married in church, but that was just a tradition. When the twins were born, I promised God we'd go to church, and we did ... for a while.

Geoff's voice came over the intercom, interrupting his thoughts. "Are you doing okay? We're about half done."

"Yep, doing okay."

When I think of it, my faith journey has been in fits and starts. The marriage retreat was a turning point when we finally understood God desires a relationship with us. That moment when Amy and I received Christ was a highlight for me. But then after Jon and Jackie left Michigan, I fell away again.

The pounding of the MRI seemed to get louder. He sighed, and the memory vanished. How long was this going to take? He tried to take a deep breath, but he couldn't relax enough to fill his lungs. Was he breathing his own exhale in this tiny tube? Squeezing his eyes tighter, he willed his mind to go back to musing.

After the twins went off to college, there had been no need to continue faking faith by attending church. Career had become the priority. Empty nesting had provided more time to work and climb farther up the ladder of success. Amy had used the extra time to jump even deeper into faith practices and tried to drag him along, which had widened the gulf between them.

He made a face as he saw things clearly for the first time ... especially his resistance to spiritual matters.

God, when Amy tried to get me to engage in faith practices, I thought she was trying to control me, so I resisted. But that meant I also resisted you.

Marriage mentoring seemed like a good solution to get the marriage back on track. At first, he and Amy had gotten into some big fights in front of their mentors. It'd been embarrassing. He would've quit, but his mentor Jim offered to meet with him alone. That worked out so much better.

Chris remembered when Jim invited him to do a Bible study together. Chris genuinely enjoyed it but made Jim promise not to let Amy know. Chris wasn't sure he would stick with it and didn't want to give Amy more ammunition to say he wasn't doing Christianity the right way.

Chris respected Jim, who was like an older version of Jon. *Jim confesses his own weaknesses, which gives me hope. He's someone who will always tell me the truth and challenge me to address my issues.*

Just then, the MRI noise paused, and Geoff came through the headphones again. "Mr. McGrath, have you fallen recently and hit your head?"

"No."

After a pause, Geoff said, "Okay. Let's keep going."

Chris's heart pounded so loud he wondered if the technician could hear it above the clamor of the MRI. *Why had Geoff asked if I fell? Had he seen something?* There had to be some reason Geoff interrupted the scan to ask that question. He tried to remember if he had fallen or hit his head recently. *No, I can't recall anything.*

There was no going back to ruminating about his faith. He considered for the hundredth time that he might have a brain tumor of some kind. Maybe even cancer. *I'm going to be okay, right God? God ... are you there?*

The noise of the MRI mercifully stopped soon after, and the table smoothly slid Chris to freedom. Geoff appeared and unhooked the cage around Chris's head, then stood back with his hand outstretched to help him up from the table. His back ached as he slowly sat up, then stood.

"We're all done now, but please remain in the waiting room after you get dressed. The radiologist needs to talk to you before you leave."

Abrupt pounding returned in his chest. *This doesn't seem normal.*

He tried to dress quickly, but his hands were shaking. He met the radiologist who was already waiting for him in the empty waiting room.

"Mr. McGrath, did you drive yourself here?"

His voice cracked. "Um ... yes, why do you ask?"

"We found you have a significant amount of fluid in your skull putting pressure on your brain. This is a dangerous situation. You must go to the ER at once. Should we get an ambulance for you, or is there someone you could call to drive you there? We cannot allow you to drive yourself."

Nausea rose suddenly within him. "My wife is only twenty minutes away. Can I call her to take me?" His legs felt unsteady beneath him, so he sat down heavily in a chair before they gave way.

"Of course. I'll be in my office." He waved toward his open door. "Let me know when she gets here." The radiologist turned and walked away.

Chris's shaking fingers managed to place a call to Amy.

Amy had sent Chris off by himself for the MRI. It didn't make sense for her to go and wait in the car. She might as well enjoy being alone with her music and her musings while she made dinner.

After connecting her phone to the Bluetooth speaker in the kitchen, she heard the soothing strains of Andrés Segovia's classical guitar music fill the room. *Ahh ... that's more like it. I need some peace today.*

She took an onion, red pepper, and a package of mushrooms out of the refrigerator, and started dicing the onion and pepper. She already had made a salad and planned to put some lamb chops on the grill once Chris returned. Glancing at the counter behind her where the fresh loaf of French bread sat, she thought some olive oil for dipping was all that was needed. Her eyes rested on a large photograph from their honeymoon hanging above the counter. They stood with arms linked on a beautiful old bridge above the Isar river in Munich. She sighed.

It was so different in the beginning of our marriage. We did everything together ... partners in every sense of the word. We dreamed about our future ... the exciting things we would do, the places we would go, and the good times we would enjoy together.

We live on easy street now since Chris has a C-Suite role at work. I appreciate our success and the perks that come with it, but it's not enough. Since the kids went away to college, something's been missing. Something's not right with us.

She sighed as she dumped the chopped onions and peppers into a frying pan then started washing the mushrooms.

She thought about how Chris always seemed distant. *He comes home from work late and plops down in front of the screen or spends hours in his "man cave" in the basement playing video games. There's never any "us" time anymore.*

She shuddered as she recalled how awkward it had been when they'd tried couples counseling.

Chris had simply leaned back in his chair with his arms crossed—his face could have been carved from stone—while she had chattered to fill in the silent stretches. He had only responded in grunts and monosyllables to the counselor's attempts at conversation. It hadn't taken long for him to quit going. It was too expensive, he'd said. *That was an excuse. We have the money. He just wouldn't invest in our marriage.*

She chopped the mushrooms with a vengeance, then dropped them into the pan with the onions and peppers. She turned on the burner and grabbed a bamboo spoon and a bottle of olive oil to sauté the mixture.

When she heard about marriage mentoring at church, she had cajoled him relentlessly until he agreed to try it.

"I'll go once. At least it's free," he'd said.

She had liked their mentors, Jim and Linda, right off the bat, and Chris had gone more than once. But she cringed now as she remembered how badly it had ended. All four of them had met, and Jim had asked them to make a list of wishes they each had for their marriage. They had to share it with each other using assertiveness and active listening.

"Remember," Jim had said, "assertiveness is one spouse asking for their wish, including how they would feel if it was granted. Active listening is the other spouse repeating back what the wish was without defensiveness or invalidating the other's feelings."

Chris had shared something from his wish list first. "I wish … I wish you would be happy to see me when I come home. I would feel welcomed and appreciated in my own home."

She remembered how anger had risen in her at his accusation. "You don't feel *welcome* in your own home? You have a ten-thousand-dollar man cave and a wife who worked full time, raised your kids, and entertained for you."

Her mentor, Linda, had spoken softly. "Amy, remember active listening is not defending yourself. Chris is sharing his feelings, which are valid for him. Can you repeat his wish and his feelings? I know this is hard, but you are learning to really listen for his feelings. That will encourage him to continue being real with you."

The wonderful aroma of the vegetables she was cooking now broke into her thoughts. Amy set the spoon down and turned off the burner.

I couldn't stand Chris embarrassing me and making me look like the bad guy. Then he got all defensive when I said I wished he would work fewer hours and plan some great dates like he used to. We never could talk without fighting, so we met with Jim and Linda individually. I don't even know if he's meeting with Jim anymore since we never talk about it.

She pushed her hair behind her ears and stared out the window as the strains of guitar music continued.

I think Linda is sweet, but she's into asking God to "speak to her" and other "spiritual exercises" that are uncomfortable to me. I sure don't want to meet her in the church prayer room to try it. What if I can't hear God? Would Linda think I'm not a real Christian? And why am I the one who needs to listen to God? What about Chris?

Her phone rang, startling her out of those dark thoughts. She left the stove to pick it up and saw Chris's photo appear. *Uh-oh. What's he calling me for? He should be home by now.* Her heart pounded an unsteady rhythm as she answered the call.

"Hey, I need a ride. They just told me I have a lot of fluid in my skull. It's putting pressure on my brain. It's an emergency. I need to go to the ER right now. They won't let me drive, even though it's around the corner. They will call an ambulance if you can't come right away."

She gasped, then said, "On my way."

March 20. Evening

Amy turned off the stove burner, grabbed the frying pan with a potholder, and shoved the still hot pan into the refrigerator. Tucking her purse under her arm, she flew out the door. At the last minute, she remembered her phone sitting on the counter and ran back to grab it. The shocking words she'd just heard from Chris's quaking voice kept circling around in her head. *A lot of fluid in my skull ... pressure on my brain ... go to the ER right away ... can't drive.*

"What the—" She slammed on the Lexus's brakes. She hadn't seen the light turn red until the last second. Her car skidded to a stop in the crosswalk, and a startled couple shot her a disapproving look as they gave her car a wide berth.

The trip to the imaging center felt like a bad dream. She skirted some traffic laws and came close to crashing several times. As she pulled up under the portico, Chris appeared from the dark shadows of the building, accompanied by a doctor. He got into the passenger seat and introduced her to the radiologist. She noticed they were both wearing surgical masks.

The doctor leaned in to talk to her. "Mrs. McGrath, I'm Dr. Collins. They're waiting for you at the ER. They already have all the images we took, so they should be fully informed. It's around the corner from here, on the north side of the hospital." He straightened up and motioned in the direction she should go.

She sped around the corner and pulled up under the ER portico. They waited a moment, but no one came out to meet them. She opened her car door just as a burly guard wearing a surgical mask marched out and yelled, "Stay in your car, ma'am."

Her heart hammered as she quickly complied.

A nurse joined the guard on Chris's side of the car, adjusting her mask as she did. They motioned for Chris to roll down his window.

The guard stopped him. "Sir, that's far enough, don't roll the window down any farther. Tell us why you are here."

"I just had a test and they said to come to the ER."

That doesn't sound urgent! Amy hijacked the conversation, leaning over him. "My husband just had an MRI at the imaging center. They found fluid in his skull, and it's pressing on his brain. They said to come here *immediately*. The images have already been transferred to your database."

The nurse grilled Chris in her muffled voice. "Sir, have you experienced a fever or chills in the past two days?"

"No."

"Any shortness of breath, cough, or difficulty breathing?"

"No."

"How about any fatigue, muscle or body aches, sore throat?"

"No."

Amy was about to lose it. "My husband's brain is about to explode or something. He needs immediate care. Why are you wasting time asking all these questions?"

"Sorry, ma'am, these questions are protocol to make sure we know if anyone coming into the hospital has the virus." The nurse addressed Chris one more time. "Is it okay if I take your temperature, sir?"

"Yes, of course."

The nurse pulled a non-contact thermometer from her pocket and pointed it at Chris's forehead. Then she slipped the thermometer back in her pocket.

"You're okay. Sir, we are going to bring you into the ER now. Do you need a wheelchair?"

"I can walk on my own."

Amy bit her lip as the nurse and guard helped her husband out of the car. Just before he exited, she grabbed her phone charger and gave it to him. She remembered being unable to enter the cardiologist's office this morning because of the virus. Would they allow her to come in the ER?

The nurse looked in at her. "I'm sorry, but no family members can accompany patients inside the hospital at this time. You will have to wait in the car. The parking lot is around to your left."

Amy shifted the car into park. "What? You've got to be kidding. He needs me to be there with him—his brain isn't right. I don't even know if he'll remember his name and other important information. There is no way I'm going to let you take him without me being there. I'm fine. I could have answered no to all those questions too. Take my temperature, you'll see." After she spit this out, she opened her door and put both feet on the pavement.

The guard quickly stepped around the car, keeping about six feet between them. "Ma'am, I'm going to have to call the police if you don't get back in your car. Hospital rules have changed, and we must protect our patients from this pandemic. You ... will ... not ... enter this building.

Please go to the parking lot. Someone will call you with an update."

She dared not defy him. She called out, "I love you, Chris," as he disappeared through the automatic doors with the nurse. She got back in the car reluctantly, turned her head away from the guard, and started toward the parking lot. She found a place to park, raised her hands to her face, and sobbed.

Unendurable moments passed, and her initial shock began to dissipate. Blinding anger and rage rose at this whole unfair situation. *They're going way too far. Their fear is out of proportion. A "pandemic"? Really? What is this, a horror movie? The news showed people in a Seattle nursing home, but they must be old, and it's probably a new strain of the seasonal flu. Besides, we're in Michigan! Talk about overreacting. He needs me. Why do I have to sit in the parking lot?*

She knew Chris wasn't a child, even though she thought he acted childish sometimes. She was passionately protective of him at this instant, yet she was totally impotent sitting outside the ER in her car while strangers diagnosed his brain problem. She screamed in frustration, baring her teeth as the scream escaped from deep within her throat. She felt like a mama bear, locked up in a cage while someone dragged off her baby to God knows where. She wanted to shake someone. But there was no one here. She was all alone.

Wait. Yo. I knew I was supposed to call her today. She fished her cell phone out of her purse. She wished she had plugged it in because her battery wasn't anywhere near full. She was glad she remembered to give Chris the charger she normally kept in her purse, but there was no way to charge her phone now until she got home. *Who knows when that will be?*

Yo didn't pick up, so she would have to leave a message. She started to speak, but tears flowed instead. All she could choke out was, "Call me, Yo. I *need* you."

Amy sat there wondering what to do next. Time stretched with the lengthening shadows. *How long will it be until someone calls me?* The parking lot lights came on, casting a sickly yellow glow over the parking lot. Glancing around at the cars parked nearby, she saw most had single occupants in them, engines running in the chilly night. *Looks like I'm not the only one in this boat. We are all in this together even though we don't know each other and can't even talk to one another.* Somehow, the thought gave her a little comfort.

She could call Linda, but she imagined her mentor would only give her biblical platitudes and tell her God was going to work this out for good. That wasn't what she was looking for. Yo was the one who would allow her to wallow in her misery and then give her practical advice.

She jumped as her cell phone rang.

"Yo, thanks for calling back." Tears started up again, and she blubbered her way through the whole sorry mess.

Yo said nothing, but her gasps and silence confirmed Amy's worst fears. This was *bad*.

"Okay, coming right over. Getting in my car as we speak. You're in the parking lot behind the main building? By the emergency room, right?"

Relief flooded Amy. "Yes, second aisle from the entrance about halfway down."

A few minutes later, she exhaled when she saw Yo's bright orange car pull up a few spaces down from her. Yo ran to the passenger side of the car and slid into the seat.

"I was so frantic. I got here as fast as I could!"

She clung to her best friend. Their long embrace was punctuated with sobs and sniffing.

"Thanks so much for coming. I feel much better just having you here with me. What should I do now?"

Yo looked her in the eye and replied, "You are doing exactly what you are supposed to do. Amy, look at me, I want you to hear this and believe it. You … are … going … to be … okay. Got it?"

She nodded, sniffling.

"First of all, my sister is a nurse. You remember Tamara, right? I called her as I drove here, and she said this pandemic thing that you've heard about is real—not a hoax. They are working their tails off in there trying to keep their patients, including Chris, safe."

"What?" She blinked, shocked.

"There's a lot we don't know yet. But you need to trust that he is in good hands. It's terrible you're out here and can't go in. I totally agree with you. I'd be furious too. But if they let you in, they must let all the other family members in too." She swept her hand across the windshield at the other cars. "And then the germs from a mysterious virus are going to multiply and spread throughout the hospital. On top of whatever Chris has, we don't want to add an unknown virus."

Amy went completely still, then closed her eyes momentarily. *It must be true because Tamara confirmed it. But a mysterious virus traveling all over the States and keeping everyone apart is so crazy. It's like a bad movie.*

"Tamara said to ask her if we have any questions after we hear from the ER doctor."

Amy let out a long, huge sigh. "Thank you so much. You don't know how much better I feel with you here." She squeezed Yo's hand. It meant the world to her to have someone to share this nightmare with. There was nothing more to do until the ER doctor called.

March 20. Night

Chris looked around the waiting room but didn't see a single person. The place was eerily quiet and empty while hospital personnel walked around wearing the protective clothing Chris had seen in movies about highly infectious diseases. He imagined his symptoms must be serious or they would have recommended he see his family doctor in the morning.

Chris sat in a wheelchair as they pushed him to a curtained examination cubicle in a large room full of cubbies, all with curtains open and beds lacking occupants. He remembered seeing the ER so full in the past that patients had lined the hallways on gurneys.

Within twenty minutes, he had been transferred to a bed and taken to another floor for a CT scan. *This is moving fast. Is it because there's no one else here? Or because I'm critically ill?*

After returning from the CT scan, a young doctor opened his curtain and entered. "Hello. I'm Dr. Peters." He shuffled several sheets of paper in his hands. "They may have told you at the imaging center that you have quite a collection of fluid within your skull. The CT scan shows the fluid is mostly old blood. We don't believe there is active bleeding. The technical term for your condition is a chronic subdural hematoma. Have you fallen or hit your head recently?"

"No, I don't remember any falls. I've had headaches for months. It's hard to remember when they started. But no car accidents, no falls, or bumps on the head that I can think of."

Dr. Peters continued. "It's okay if you can't come up with a specific mishap to trigger this. The blood looks like it's old, so it could have been a little bump that bled slowly over a long period of time. The collection is significant, about an inch thick and the size of a man's hand. It covers three lobes of your brain. It's certainly headache worthy. We're going to admit you to the intensive care unit. Tomorrow, they'll do another CT scan, and the neurosurgeon will be here to see you. It is possible you may have surgery tomorrow. It will be a little while before they take you to your room. Do you have any questions?"

Chris's stomach growled loudly. "I'm starving, can I get something to eat?"

"I'm sorry, but all you can have is clear liquids. We need to make sure your stomach is empty in case you have surgery in the morning. I can get you some apple juice, though."

Chris nodded. At least it was something.

After the doctor left, Chris groaned. He had hoped for a simple solution such as "take two of these pills, go home, and call your doctor in the morning."

I'm glad he didn't mention the word "tumor." But a large collection of old blood sounds nasty. What could have caused the bleed? Has my lousy diet and lack of exercise finally caught up with me? Is this my fault?

His diet had been a point of contention with Amy. The more she criticized, the more he withdrew or deflected with sarcastic humor. He often joked that his family's food triangle consisted of butter, salt, sugar, and anything you could put butter, salt, or sugar on. As an executive who worked long hours, he rationalized his sedentary life. *Was she right? Will I have to give up my food triangle joke forever?*

His thoughts turned to what might be next. *What kind of surgery? I should have asked. Of all the crazy times to get sick, how in the world did I manage to do it at the beginning of a pandemic?*

He reached up and massaged his head, shutting his eyes against the throbbing. With his eyes closed, the pain only intensified. There was no TV to distract him. The ER was mercifully quiet with no other patients around, but what could he do while waiting around for a room? He had to distract himself somehow. His thoughts returned to his ruminating in the MRI tube before Geoff interrupted him. *Where was I? Oh, yes. The Bible study with Jim.*

The study had helped him recognize hurdles in his life. Areas where he believed lies about himself.

My life has been all about achievement from the moment I left the U.P. and my family's dysfunction behind. I thought I had to make a lot of money so I would have a better life than my parents and gain the respect of my wife. Performance became my identity. But Jim said that even without my job, I'm still a valuable person—the man God created me to be.

He suddenly panicked. *When will I be able to get back to work? What will my team think about me? I don't want anyone else to take my job. What would I do if I lost my position? Will Jezebel be safe until Amy can get her home?*

As the automatic blood pressure cuff abruptly squeezed his arm, he caught himself. *Wait ... I was thinking about how the Bible study was revealing the performance-based hurdles in my life. But I jumped right back into worrying about them.*

He chuckled softly. *Guilty as charged. Well, I prayed for help to understand how the things I was learning apply to me. I see I have a lot of work to do to break my habits. But as Jim said, so does everyone else.*

In the parking lot, Amy's car stayed warm as she and Yo sat and talked about inconsequential things. They both jumped when her cell phone rang. She picked it up. "Hello?"

Yo fished a pad of paper and a pen out of her purse, motioning for Amy to put the call on speaker.

"Mrs. McGrath? This is Dr. Peters. I'm an ER doctor. I'm sorry you can't be here, but we're taking good care of Mr. McGrath. He has already had a CT scan. We have examined him and consulted with a neurosurgeon."

Amy was grateful Yo was taking notes. "Thank you, Dr. Peters. What have you found out?"

Dr. Peter's voice was crisp. "The CT scan showed Mr. McGrath has a large collection of what appears to be old blood pressing on his brain—a chronic subdural hematoma. We are admitting him to the ICU and will monitor him all night. In the morning, we'll do another CT scan. The neurosurgeon will be in to see him as well. Your husband may be having surgery tomorrow to remove the hematoma. Do you have any questions?"

"Dr. Peters, I *must* be allowed in to be with Chris. Possible surgery tomorrow on his brain? I *must* see him before you do surgery. I'm fine. No sniffles or cough or anything. You can take my temp—"

The doctor cut her off, his voice kind, but firm. "I'm sorry. I'm sure this is awfully hard on you. I assure you if we thought it was safe to let family members in, we would.

People can have the virus and yet have no symptoms. On top of your husband's condition, you certainly don't want to add this virus. If you are still in the parking lot, you might want to go home now. He is in good hands."

Dr. Peter's voice softened. "The neurosurgeon will call you tomorrow with more details once he has seen your husband. Feel free to call the hospital at any time for updates. I don't know what room he'll be in yet, but Mr. McGrath said he'll call to let you know. Good night, Mrs. McGrath."

She softened her voice in response to his. "Thank you, Dr. Peters. Goodbye."

After disconnecting the phone, she reached out to Yo and gripped her hand, breaking down in heaving sobs. When her tears had subsided a bit, Yo promised to call her tomorrow and got back in her own car. Amy maneuvered out of the parking lot, barely able to see through her watery vision.

Chris had never been in an ICU. His single room was spacious. There was a little glass-enclosed office off to one side, and he could see the office also had glass on the other side of it, facing another ICU room. This allowed one nurse to watch two ICU patients at once. The room was mercifully quiet and had subdued lighting.

Wow, this is overkill. I'm sure I don't need all this. Heck, I drove myself to the MRI a few hours ago. But it sure is nice and quiet.

As soon as he was settled, he called Amy. He wanted to give her his room number and then get to sleep.

She answered right away. "Oh, I'm glad you called. I'm just driving home now. I've been so miserable waiting to hear from you. Did you see I tried to get into the ER after you? The rude guard bullied me back into my car. He threatened to call the police. I was furious. I haven't heard any shutdown commands from the governor. How insane that they won't let me in to see you. And did they tell you they may do surgery tomorrow? Did you ask them what they will be doing in the surgery? How are you anyway?"

He had moved the phone away from his ear as her sharp voice intensified his headache. After waiting patiently for her to finish, he spoke slowly and quietly. "I'm okay. I'm exhausted and starving. I can't have any food because they might do surgery tomorrow. I don't know exactly what kind of surgery. I just got into my room—it's 4231. I heard the governor gave some specific rules to the hospitals about visitors which they must follow."

"Well, I never heard about the governor's rules. Who told you?"

"My nurse." His voice was getting weaker in his exhaustion. He knew he wouldn't be able to change Amy's mind once she had launched into a tirade, so he changed topics.

"It would be a good idea for you to get some masks and start wearing them when you leave the house. You should see the lengths they're going to in here. It's like something from a disaster movie. Based on what I've seen, this seems unlikely to be going away soon."

He heard her scoff through the phone. "This will blow over before long. It's not that serious."

How can she say that, especially after what we just went through? She was behaving childishly, and her opinion could be dangerous. They each tried a few more times to make their points, but their disagreement escalated.

Finally, she yelled, "I will not buy any masks, and that's my final word."

He was exhausted, stressed, and couldn't deal with more arguing. Their goodbyes were brief.

I don't need this sort of drama. Can't she stop even once to put aside her inconvenience and think about what I am facing right now? He wanted to pout and complain, but there was no one to listen. He folded his arms across his stomach to ease the knot forming there. But that didn't help either. When he was too tired to be annoyed with her behavior any longer, he plugged his phone into the charger, rolled over, and eventually fell asleep.

It was late when Amy finally returned home. Her head throbbed, her body ached all over, and her eyes burned from crying. She felt like she had been assaulted and left for dead. The memory of her argument with Chris still smarted. After staring numbly in the refrigerator, she decided to ignore the healthy dinner she'd started earlier—it seemed like years ago. A cold bottle of water and a bag of chips from the pantry was all she wanted as she trudged upstairs.

She tossed the bag of chips on the bed and changed into her pajamas. There were tons of people she should call right now, but she felt too drained. The calls would have to wait until morning.

She thought back through the day's events. Then she remembered her own harrowing trip to the ER when the twins were born. Chris had been a hero, springing into action to be her advocate. *Could I be his advocate now? How can I do that if I can't be with him? There must be something I can do.* She found a scrap of paper and a pencil in her nightstand and scribbled down some ideas.

Satisfied, she turned on the TV. A mindless diversion at this late hour was the only chance she had of falling asleep tonight.

When Love Multiplied— Twenty-Two Years Ago

Amy lay in bed, her hands on her swollen belly. It felt like the twins inside of her were competing in a wrestling match. Chris was already gone for the day, and she was grateful he worked flex hours so he could be home with her in the early afternoon. After thirty-two weeks, she had pregnancy-induced hypertension, but she wasn't worried. Her blood pressure seemed under control so far, and she was already on leave from work and kept off her feet as much as possible. Thankfully, she wasn't on full bed rest, but she did enjoy sleeping in and taking it easy.

I feel a little nauseated. I wonder if it was that rich dinner last night. Amy gently massaged her belly, wondering which infant she was touching. One of them jabbed her in their tight confines. *I can't wait to hold them in my arms. What will they look like?* Amy raised her knees up to relieve her aching back and drifted off to sleep again.

Chris gently shook his wife's shoulder. "Amy! Wake up!" No response. "Amy!" His heart pounded and his gut wrenched.

Finally, he saw her eyes open. They were glazed as she stared up at him.

"Amy, can you hear me?"

"Uh, yeah." She grimaced. "I must have slept in. What time is it?"

"It's noon. I called you three times. You didn't pick up, so I came home. Do you feel okay?" He pressed his hand to her forehead. It felt hot.

"It hurts here." She pointed to her right side. "And I feel sick. Maybe I need some water." She rolled to her side and tried to sit up but fell back down. "Gah, I'm dizzy. I think I'm going to be sick."

He panicked and ran to the bathroom to get a cool, wet towel. "Here, put this on your head. I'll get you a bowl. We better take your blood pressure." He knew he was talking loud and fast but couldn't stop himself. He wiped beads of sweat from his forehead and hurried from the bedroom.

He came back with a bowl and the blood pressure cuff. Wrapping the cuff around her limp arm was difficult because his hands were shaking, and Amy had fallen asleep again. He noticed her hand was puffy and swollen. *This is serious.*

"Amy! Wake up." He shook her gently again, and she opened her eyes. He set the cuff down. "I'm going to call an ambulance. You have some symptoms they told us to watch for. Hang in there, babe. You're going to be okay."

Twenty minutes later, Chris let in the emergency crew and watched them lift his wife onto a gurney. After making sure she was stable, they moved toward the door and the waiting ambulance.

As soon as the ambulance pulled away, Chris raced to the garage so he could follow. His hands shook on the steering wheel, and his teeth chattered. *God, this can't be happening. God, please. Save Amy. Please don't let her die! God, I promise I'll do anything you want. Please God!*

When he arrived at the hospital, they were prepping Amy for an emergency C-section. He was sent off to a changing room to put on scrubs, a cap, and a mask to join her. He busted out of the changing room, tying the drawstring on his pants as he dashed down the hallway.

He entered the room and was shocked at the sight of his wife. Her face looked pale, and her eyes were closed once more. The nurses had strapped both her arms down and stuck one with an IV. They put him into a chair with wheels so he could be rolled out of the way should he pass out. *No way are they going to make me leave.* He sat at her side, holding one hand as best he could. He clenched his jaw, determined to stay conscious.

He whispered close to Amy's ear and squeezed her hand. "I'm here, babe. I'm right here. I'm not going anywhere. We can do this." He was relieved when her eyes popped open.

"Yes, we can." Amy turned her head and smiled. Her dimples were there, but he saw tears in the corners of her eyes.

Once the spinal injection had taken effect, and she had no feeling from the waist down, the staff set up a drape in front of Amy's abdomen to shield the gruesome details of the surgery from view. Now Chris only saw the heads of the obstetrician and her staff as they bent over their work.

A few minutes later, the doctor said, "You have a baby boy." Chris saw a tiny pink baby in the doctor's arms, his little face still and quiet. A few moments later he saw the second baby. "And a girl!" She was even tinier than their boy and just as quiet. The babies were whisked away to the other side of the room to be cleaned up and evaluated. Chris craned his neck to see what was happening, but the nurses were in the way. After what seemed like an eternity, he heard a faint whimper from one of the babies.

"I hear one of them crying, that's a good sign," Chris whispered to Amy. He had to remember to breathe, waiting to hear a cry from the second baby. Finally, he heard it. A weak cry, but a cry, nonetheless. The whimper sounded like a little bird.

Amy burst into tears, and he fought his own back.

He squeezed her hand. "Did you hear that? You did it, babe. We're parents!"

Whew ... Amy's okay ... babies are okay. We got this. Right, God?

Amy couldn't wait to bring her babies home after three weeks in the neonatal intensive care unit. The twins, Brad and Michelle, were finally thriving sufficiently to leave the hospital. As the nurse wheeled Amy out the door, she gasped at the long limo awaiting them. Chris stood nearby with a bouquet of flowers.

"Chris, I'm impressed you rented a limo for the drive home. Take a picture of it, though, because I'm sure the gesture will be lost on the twins until they are much older."

"Are you kidding?" Chris said. "This is for you, babe. You've been incredible through all of this, and I couldn't be prouder of you. No matter what challenges are ahead, we'll conquer them together."

Amy felt so loved in that moment.

"I have a clear weekend ahead of me to get the kids on a schedule before I go back to work on Monday."

But by Sunday, both Amy and Chris were exhausted. When one baby slept, the other was awake. When one screamed, the other woke and screamed as well. If one was hungry, the other was hungry too. Trying to keep them fed, changed, clean, and calm was nonstop work, day and night. When Chris had to go back to work—after using up all his vacation and sick days—Amy knew she couldn't do it alone.

Chris arranged for Amy's mom to stay with them for two weeks, and his mom agreed to come the two weeks after that. Their nanny would start work after the first month. That would give Amy time to set up the schedule before her maternity leave ended, and she went back to work.

The night before Chris had to return, Amy shifted uncomfortably in the bed. No matter what position she was in, something hurt. She finally settled on her back. Chris turned toward her and rubbed her shoulder.

"I'll call you every chance I get tomorrow," Chris promised. "I know you'll do well with your mom here to help."

"I hope so."

"Can I do anything to help you sleep? Foot rub?"

"No, I'm just fidgety. Keep talking. My body will settle down soon."

"Well, I'll do my best." Chris paused for a moment. "You know, you are the most amazing woman in the world. I know I keep saying that, but it's true."

"Mm-hmm."

"Our babies are so incredible. I can't even believe I'm a dad. I bet they'll have your good looks and brains. They'll be successful at everything they do." Amy stayed silent but loved hearing Chris being so upbeat and positive.

"I know it's a lot of work now, but I can't even tell you how grateful I am that all three of you are fine. When you were in the ambulance, I was scared sick." His voice choked up and she rolled over to face him.

She put her hand on his cheek.

"I couldn't bear losing you. I would probably ... well, I'm thankful I don't have to think about that."

She swallowed back tears. "I was ... I was terrified I would lose the babies."

He cleared his throat. "You know I don't often pray. But I prayed hard when I was following the ambulance. I *couldn't* lose you. I promised God I would do anything if he saved you."

Amy moved her hand to his shoulder in the dark room. "You did? I'm glad you prayed for us." She knew Chris had struggled in his walk with God, and she felt a spark of hope at his confession.

They both grew silent, his thumb stroking her cheek.

"Uh, Amy, I need to keep my promise to God. I'm not sure how. But maybe when the twins are older, we could go to church. Maybe that will show God I am truly grateful. What do you think?"

She snuggled closer. "I like that. I was raised in church, and I would like to raise our kids in church too."

"Oh good." He exhaled. "We can find one later. I love you so much."

He gently tipped her face to his, and they shared a lingering kiss.

March 21. Morning

Ding. Then a second later, another *Ding.* Amy's sleeping brain nagged she needed to respond to something. She sat up, looking groggily around her, not sure where the noise had come from but knowing it was important. Her awareness came into sharp focus once it dawned on her that Chris wasn't next to her. He was in the ICU. And he was supposed to have brain surgery today.

Where's my phone? She frantically searched among the bedcovers, remembering she hadn't plugged it in last night. Finally, she found it under the covers.

Punching in her security code, she noted the battery power was at 9 percent.

Chris had texted her.

> **CHRIS:** Hey bab going for a ct scan in a mintue. Pain horibel. Level ten. luv u

He wasn't the best at spelling, but this was ridiculous. *Is he worse this morning? Pain level at a ten?* Her head hung thinking about how she ended the call last night. She texted back.

> **AMY:** Glad to hear from you. Let me know when you get back. Need to talk. Love ya.

That little positive act helped her smile. She threw on her robe, her head filled with a whirlwind of thoughts.

Noticing a crumpled bit of paper on the nightstand, she remembered the list she'd made last night. Picking it up, she read the list. *Take notes ... Ask questions ... Be positive.* A good list. A notebook would help her take notes and record the answers to her questions. She would try to be positive. Hopefully, she could see Chris today. She plugged in her phone and made a cup of black coffee with their bedroom coffee maker. The phone rang. Chris.

She eagerly answered. "How are you?"

"Not good. This is the worst pain I've ever felt. They gave me some meds for the pain, which make me foggy even though they don't seem to be working. Didn't sleep well last night."

"I didn't sleep well either ... this is a lot to deal with. Besides the pain, are you okay?"

"I'm tired of being here already. Everything moves at a snail's pace. I still haven't had anything to eat. I haven't seen the surgeon yet. I know they're doing their best, but I have work to do, and I don't have time for this."

She bit her lip. There was nothing she could do except follow her list—ask questions and be positive.

"You've had two CT scans now, are they as awful as an MRI?"

"No, they're quicker than an MRI. Also, you don't have to enter a long tunnel, so no claustrophobia."

"Is it uncomfortable?"

"Let me put it this way. It's no memory foam mattress."

"Is it noisy?"

"Yes, but not as noisy as an MRI."

"That's good." She tried to think of something else to say.

Thankfully, he filled the silence. "They won't let me get up. Say I'm a fall risk. But I've been walking until now without falling."

She teased him. "Oh, so you have pretty nurses at your beck and call?"

"Uh, one's a man. Not pretty. And I'd like to go to the bathroom by myself."

She laughed—grateful she had managed to get him talking. She felt calmer knowing he was responding to her questions—a good sign to her this fluid hadn't damaged his brain so far.

When they hung up, she thought about the time when the twins were born, and Chris prayed for them. She knew God had answered Chris's prayers and kept her twins safe. Sending up a quick prayer for her husband now, she hoped God would answer. She pulled the crumpled list out of her pocket and wrote a fourth item—*pray*.

Then she sprinted into action, brushing her teeth and putting on nice clothes. More makeup than usual helped disguise her lack of sleep. No telling when the neurosurgeon would call, but she wanted to be ready to appear at the hospital doors this morning. This time, she could bypass the ER. They had to let her in if they were doing surgery on him today.

She grabbed her phone and headed down the stairs, then plugged it in again. Opening a few drawers in the kitchen, she found the unused notebook she was looking for. She prepared her breakfast of champions, oatmeal with cinnamon and raisins. As she stood at the kitchen counter shoveling spoons of hot cereal into her mouth, she jotted down a to-do list for the day.

I need to let everyone know he's in the hospital—his parents, my parents, and our sisters. And of course, the twins.

Ding. A text from Yo.

Yo: Are you up?

AMY: Yep—Chris texted, and we talked already. He had another CT scan this morning. Doc hasn't called yet.

YO: My sis says Dr. Matthews is the best in the Neuro department, so ask for him. Call you later, gotta run.

She gave the last message a thumbs-up emoji, then put down the phone.

As she finished the last spoon of oatmeal, her phone rang.

"Mrs. McGrath, this is Dr. Matthews from the neurosurgery department. I've just visited your husband and reviewed the MRI from last night as well as the two CT scans. Do you have time now for me to discuss his case?"

"Yes, absolutely." She sat down at the table, relieved to hear from the surgeon Tamara had recommended.

"We've found he has a chronic subdural hematoma on the left side of his skull."

"Can you explain what that means in layman's terms?"

"Of course. A chronic subdural hematoma is an encapsulated collection of blood and fluid on the surface of the brain. Chronic means it has been building up slowly over time. The brain has a thick, fibrous membrane surrounding it called the dura which protects the brain. The blood and fluid are sitting directly between the dura and the brain. It's on the left side, and it's quite large. Dr. Peters may have told you it's about an inch thick and the size of a man's hand. It covers three lobes of his brain and is shifting the centerline of his brain from the left to the right by about one-fourth of an inch. I understand your husband has been having headaches for some time?"

"Yes, he has. But wait a minute, let me get this straight. It's the size of a man's hand? With a build-up so large, what has it done to his brain? How could this have gone on so long? He has been having headaches for months. We've been to several doctors, he's had a cardiological work-up, and he's only recently been asked to have an MRI."

Dr. Matthews hesitated for a moment. "Most of the time, a hematoma is caused by a fall or a blow to the head. Mr. McGrath told me he doesn't remember falling or hitting his head recently. His doctor may have asked him the same question, but they would not have pursued it further if he didn't recall an injury. Unless you remember an incident, it could be this hematoma is a bit unusual, not something a family doctor would normally recognize or even test for. Mr. McGrath told my PA—sorry, that's my physician assistant—he was taking a baby aspirin as a preventive measure. I have seen one case where a spontaneous brain bleed occurred in a man his age who was taking a daily baby aspirin."

Amy switched the phone to speaker and laid it down on the table so she could take notes. "That makes sense. Go on."

"The blood had been slowly accumulating for some time, which allowed the brain to adapt and accommodate the fluid. It is likely he didn't show symptoms until the fluid collection was sizable. Mr. McGrath told me his primary care physician asked him to do the 'drunk walk.' That was an innovative way to diagnose the situation. I understand it was the PCP who sent him in for the MRI. She may have saved his life."

Amy sighed. "I still think someone should have suggested this months ago. But now, what is your plan of action?"

"We'll be testing and watching your husband over the weekend, looking for any changes in the size of the hematoma. Sometimes these things will begin to resolve themselves. We do know the size hasn't changed from last night to this morning, and it looks like there is no new blood. Your husband is what we refer to as a 'stable bleeder.' We will also be testing for possible causes of the hematoma—for instance, blood clotting problems or a possible spinal fluid leak. If things don't begin to resolve themselves, I would expect we'll have to do surgery in two days, on Monday."

She was busily taking notes as the doctor spoke. She didn't have time to process any of this information, but robotically copied down his comments. "And the surgery?"

"It's called a craniotomy. We make an incision in his scalp from his left ear to his forehead in the shape of a large question mark. Then we peel back his scalp and use a cranial drill to make three holes in his skull. Next, we cut through the bone to connect these holes so we can remove the bone flap by carefully separating it from the dura. That gives us access to evacuate the hematoma and encapsulating membrane. At the end, we put the bone flap back using titanium plates and screws, then we stitch his scalp back in place. It's quite common. I do about seventy-five of these a year. Usually, the patients are much older than your husband. If we do surgery Monday, you could expect him home by Friday."

"My God, that surgery is just the most horrible thing I could imagine. Can I come in to be with my husband?"

"I believe they will still allow you to come in the day of the surgery. As of today, they will only allow one family member. And I can't guarantee anything at this point. If our virus patients keep increasing at the rate they are now, things can change. Every day, we receive notices with new instructions to follow due to the pandemic. One benefit of having the shutdown of elective surgeries is I can schedule this surgery any day or time I want. The operating rooms are at 10 percent of their normal capacity. I wish I could give you more, but trust me, there are good reasons for the hospital's caution."

"If you don't mind me asking, how long have you been doing these surgeries? Where were you educated?"

Dr. Matthews gave her a rundown of his thirteen years' experience. He shared his background, schooling, and his passion for helping patients.

She sighed once more. "I guess I'll have to accept all this. What about his prognosis? What are the risks?" She sat with pen poised above the notebook.

"Because of the location of the hematoma, he could come out of surgery with speech problems or motor problems on the right side. You may not have known, but the left side of the brain controls motor function on the right side of the body. Most people have a full recovery eventually. He will probably need some physical therapy after the surgery and speech therapy as well. It could take up to a year for a full recovery."

The news seemed like too much for her to process. Just yesterday, she and Chris were living their normal lives. Of course, there was fighting and conflict and avoidance, but it was normal. Suddenly nothing in their lives seemed "normal."

"Mrs. McGrath, I know this must be shocking and overwhelming to you," the surgeon said, seemingly understanding her thoughts. "But I'll contact you regularly with updates. If you have any questions, call my office, and they will reach me anytime. I will return your calls whenever I am able. I want you to know I am personally monitoring your husband and will do everything in my power to see he comes through this as healthy as possible. You are not alone. I'm here for both you and your husband."

She felt the pent-up tension inside of her break apart and dissolve. Unexpectedly, a lump rose in her throat. "Thank you, Doctor."

After they ended the call, she sat numbly and stared at the wall. Her mind roared like a hurricane, and her heart pounded wildly. She wanted to run, scream, cry, do *something*, but she couldn't move. Then something Dr. Matthews said about baby aspirin struck her.

I told Chris he should be taking a baby aspirin because of his family history of heart attacks. Of all the health advice I've given him, I can't believe this is the only one he followed. What if I caused this?

She dropped her head on her arms and cried out. "Oh God, help! Help me. Help Chris. Our entire world has turned upside down, and I can't do anything. I'm so scared." Hot tears soaked her sleeves, and her shoulders heaved with sobs.

After a while, her heart calmed, and her mind stopped spinning. She lifted her head and wiped her face. She took a deep breath and exhaled raggedly. *God will see us through this. He must.*

March 21. Afternoon

Amy spent the rest of the day calling and texting family and friends. Everyone was shocked and dismayed to hear the news. Michelle and Brad wanted to come home from college immediately, but their area had no virus cases, so it seemed safer for them to stay put.

She called her parents, anticipating her dad would want to come and stay with her. "Thanks, Dad, but I don't want to take a chance on any of us getting this virus. I need to stay healthy for Chris, and I would feel horrible if you or Mom got it from me."

Amy could hear her mom's voice quaver when they talked. She wished they could share a big hug.

Amy felt bad having to call her mother-in-law, Sharon, with such horrible news. She bit her lip when she heard the concern in Sharon's sweet voice. The older woman promised to keep up her weekly Sunday dinners for the twins, and if their college closed, they would move in with her. Amy hugged herself, reassured that her kids were close to loving family.

Next on her list was her father-in-law, Chuck. She could count on one hand the number of times she had spoken to him. But she felt it was the right thing to do. Her conversation was cordial but short, and she was surprised at the warmth in his voice. He offered to help in any way he could.

Everyone's emotional reactions made her even more anxious and worried.

The call she saved for last was to Linda. She felt sheepish that she'd ended their dinner at the café abruptly, but she imagined Linda would feel bad if she were left out. With all the other names crossed off her list, she found her marriage mentor's name in her contacts and pressed call. *Last one, then I get a rest.*

Linda's voice radiated warmth. "Hello, Amy. I was just thinking about you. How are you doing?"

Amy was surprised when she suddenly choked up, and she struggled to sound normal. "Well, I guess you could say I'm not doing well, but much better than Chris is." Her vision blurred and she blinked hard. She went on to describe what happened since the day before, feeling like it had been about a month instead of a single day.

Linda remained silent through the explanation, then said, "Oh, my goodness. I can't imagine all the emotions you're dealing with, and Chris too. Wow. I don't have any answers for you, but I want you to know Jim and I are here for you no matter what. Call any time—day or night. We'll organize a prayer team if you want us to."

Just hearing Linda's voice was calming and reassuring. Suddenly, Amy felt less drained. "Thank you so much, Linda. Yes, please do ask people to pray. I'm not sure what to do. The worst part is, I can't be there with him."

"Oh, I wish I could be there to give you a hug. But *you* must feel much worse since you can't give Chris a hug. You can't be together, and your friends and family need to stay away because of the virus. This is an incredibly difficult time to be alone. Focus on what you *can* do. What is your next step? What can I do to help? Do you need a meal?"

"I'm good with food, but maybe I'll need help when Chris gets home." She rubbed her forehead. "Focus on what I can do? My next step? What in the world would that be?"

"When I don't know what to do, I usually clean the house." Linda laughed. "I know it sounds weird, but when I'm working, it clears my head. For you, it may be taking a walk or listening to music. Or soaking in a warm bath. Do whatever works for you to still your mind from the chaos. Take a mental step away. Sometimes just being in silence helps us figure out what we should do. I can only imagine what you are feeling. But I don't have to imagine what God is feeling. He wants to strengthen and calm you so you can fight this battle. You don't have to do it alone, Amy."

Amy exhaled. "Thank you, Linda. You don't know what this means to me."

Linda prayed for her and Chris before hanging up.

After assuring herself she'd called all the pertinent people, Amy drew a hot bubble bath and slipped in with a sigh. Scooting down so the water rose to her neck, she unwound as the warmth enveloped her. Thinking back to her conversation with Linda, she was glad her mentor would organize a prayer team. Having a bunch of super-spiritual people asking God to help them felt reassuring.

Super-spiritual ... where have I heard that before? She added more hot water to warm the tub. *Oh yes, it was that time Chris called me super-spiritual.* She grimaced, remembering the day three or four years ago. She had gotten off work a little early and had spent the late afternoon with some church friends at the park for a mini retreat. Chris had come home early from work to surprise her, but she wasn't home. She had walked in later feeling refreshed, but Chris had greeted her with a scowl on his face.

"Where have you been? I got off early to surprise you, but I was surprised instead. I'm starving, and I don't see any dinner." Chris raised his eyebrows and held out his hands.

She'd tried to defuse the situation. "Sorry. I didn't know you would be early today. I was at a mini retreat. I've got leftovers, so it won't take long to warm up dinner."

Grabbing a few containers from the refrigerator, she had opened them and dumped the food onto plates. "This afternoon was so amazing." She spoke over her shoulder as she worked. "One of the women from church talked to us about memorizing Scripture. She quoted the whole book of James to us. I want us to do that together." She had turned to catch his eye.

Chris's frown had deepened. "Count me out. There's no way I'm going to become *super-spiritual* like you, spouting Bible verses at people. Why are you always trying to get me to do more at church? I guess I'm not holy enough for you." He had turned toward the basement door and disappeared behind it.

Amy had stood there fuming. Why was he so stubborn? Her other friends had husbands who were involved in church. Why wouldn't he join her? How many times had she asked? Predictably, the next day Chris had appeared after work with a bouquet of flowers. She had thrown them in the garbage. Flowers were not going to cut it with her ever again.

That had been the end of him going to church with her. She had spent the last several years alone on Sunday mornings.

The cooling water and her wrinkled fingertips interrupted her train of thought and prompted her to get dressed. As she reapplied her makeup, she recalled having dinner at Tabikh with Linda a few days ago.

At the time, Amy didn't think Linda's story of how her marriage had changed applied to her marriage at all. But now her mentor's words came back to her. "For me, it wasn't about what I needed to do. I had to learn who God created me to be. He didn't intend for me to be a control freak."

Amy paused with the mascara brush in her hand. *Is that what I am? A control freak? That doesn't sound very attractive. I must admit I do feel superior to Chris, because I'm active at church, and he isn't. But I just want the best for us. When Chris said he wanted to be all in for God, I assumed he would jump in with me to volunteer and study the Bible. But the more I pushed him, the more he resisted. Then he stopped going altogether. Did I push him away from church? God, I don't want to be a control freak, especially if that means pushing my husband away from you.*

She needed to find something to do. All this time waiting was causing her to rethink everything. As she caught up with paperwork, her phone rang again.

"Hey. How was your day?" Yo asked. "Sorry I didn't get back to you sooner. It's been a day, but probably not as bad as yours." Her voice was businesslike and efficient, as usual.

"It's good to hear from you. I had a day of talking, and I'm pretty talked out. I called all the family and lots of friends. Chris was in horrible pain this morning, but he's doing better now. I did get to talk to the surgeon who was assigned to him. He seemed nice. You won't believe this, but it's Dr. Matthews, the same doc Tamara told you about."

"That's great. She told me everyone raves about him. He has implemented some groundbreaking techniques in the neurosurgery field."

Once more, Amy felt a sense of peace. "Good to know. Thanks for checking."

"I have more to tell you. I asked Tamara about the pandemic and all the rules. She said they are implementing plans which had only been on paper up to now. Plans for a worldwide pandemic. Personal protective equipment is being worn by all staff who are around pandemic patients—gowns, face masks, eye protection, hairnets, the whole shebang. She confirmed no one is being let into the hospital for visitation. She also said the number of cases coming in during the last few days has been rising exponentially. They are running out of space in the dedicated pandemic ICUs."

Amy gasped as Yo continued.

"Hospital administration is wondering if the system will be able to handle all the cases if it keeps up at this pace. They are also running out of ventilators. You need to wear a mask when you go out. You need to keep yourself healthy for when Chris comes home."

Amy gripped the phone. "Wow, this is surreal. Suddenly, we find out Chris has a mysterious brain problem right as a pandemic hit?" She shook her head. It was a relief to have Yo's help, but now she felt even more anxious and sick to her stomach. "Yo, thank you so, so much. I don't know what I would do without you. But I need to go now. I haven't eaten all day and my stomach is protesting."

"I'm not surprised, girlfriend. If you look on your front porch, I left a package for you just before I called. Don't get excited—I didn't cook. It's carryout from Tabikh. And some masks. Get some rest. I'll call you tomorrow. I'm glad to help in any way I can."

"What a sweet surprise. Love you, friend."

Amy retrieved the bag from her porch and wolfed down the delicious meal. For dessert, she dipped her finger into a jar of chocolate spread she found in her cupboard. Then she sank down onto the sofa, clicked on the TV, and promptly fell asleep.

When Love Dimmed—
Ten Years Ago

Chris felt the cool breeze of late September ruffling his hair as he sat on the bleachers watching his son Brad running back and forth across the soccer field. He shook his head, marveling at how fast both the twins had overcome their premature start at life. Starting kindergarten at age six helped, and they'd never looked back. Their soccer skills had steadily developed through the levels of peewee to upper elementary. He raised his arms and cheered as Brad took a shot and got past the goalkeeper. *That's my boy.*

Amy approached, scanning the crowd for him. He raised his arm and waved at her. She climbed up and sat down, giving him a quick side hug.

"Whew, I'm tired and it's only early afternoon." She spoke to Chris, but her eyes were traveling back and forth with Brad on the field. "I got all the groceries and ordered the cake for the big birthday bash. I can't wait to surprise them. Did you hear from your mom? Is she coming?"

"Yep. Mom and Carrie are both coming. I think the twins will be so surprised. I never had birthday parties growing up. I'm glad we can do this for them. Twelve is an important age in a kid's life. Can you believe they'll be in middle school this year?"

Amy shook her head. "Nope. It's crazy how fast time has gone. Seems like our lives get busier and busier." She clapped and cheered as Brad stole the ball from the other team. "Speaking of busy, the kids will be able to join the youth group at church. They meet on Sunday nights and have all sorts of great trips and camps lined up. I think they'll love it."

He turned to look at her, tension tightening his gut. "I don't know about that. Sunday nights are family time, and this year homework will be a bigger issue. You know Michelle still needs extra time to keep up. They get plenty of social development from soccer, and this year they're playing on separate teams too. That means more time our family will spend apart. We should hold off on the youth group thing." He turned back to the game, leaning his forearms on his knees and intently watching. He heard her exasperated sigh but pretended not to.

The Sunday afternoon after the kids' big birthday bash, Amy went for a run while Michelle was playing at a friend's house and Chris and Brad were bonding in the basement. Chris called the basement his *man cave,* which annoyed her. When would she get a *she shed?* The dark paneled room in their basement included a dart board, video games displayed on a massive 8K TV, custom gaming chairs, Razer headsets, a punching bag, reclining home theater seats with cup holders, and phone charging ports—the envy of every man who saw it. Amy considered the basement her rival, and she had given up trying to compete.

Chris makes me so mad. He knew I didn't want Brad to have more video games—I made that clear—but he got one for Brad's birthday anyway. They've been holed up in a dark basement all weekend killing people with their controllers.

She reached the end of the street and turned into Rochester Park. As she pounded the pavement, she saw people enjoying the warm sunshine.

A young boy went by on a bike, followed by a man who called out to him, "Whoa, look at you go!" The young boy chortled happily at the progress he was making.

By the edge of the pond, four boys about Brad's age were fishing. One of them reeled in a tiny fish, and they all laughed.

A young family sat at a picnic table, playing a board game.

As she rounded a corner, she heard her name called out. She stopped to see Pam Ito waving from the other side of the pond. Pam's son Jason was Brad's best friend.

"Hey, Pam. How's it going?" Amy jogged up to the other woman.

"It's going well. You're certainly energetic. I can't remember the last time I ran anywhere."

"I love to run. It clears my head." She didn't want to share what she was clearing her head from.

"Awesome. Hey, did you know youth group starts tonight at church? I'm taking Jason. He said Brad might want to go. I would be glad to pick up Michelle too."

Amy thought about Chris's mention of "family time," but he'd been holed up all day with Brad. "Hmm. Let me ask the kids. I'd love to see them join the youth group. I could bring them all home."

"Okay, let me know. It starts at seven."

Amy turned toward home and started jogging again. With every step, she felt a plan coming together. Just this morning at church, Michelle had given her a flyer about the youth group. She said all her friends were going to be there. Brad had been quiet about it, but if he knew Jason were going, he'd probably want to attend. Why shouldn't she arrange for them to go? Chris was against it because of family time, but how was playing video games with Brad family time when it was only half the family?

As she opened the door and stepped into the kitchen, Brad was getting a soda from the refrigerator.

"Hi, Mom. Dad and I are playing my new video game. It's super awesome." He turned to go back downstairs.

"Hey, before you go back down, I saw Mrs. Ito in the park just now. She said Jason is going to check out the youth group at church tonight. If you're up for it, she'll pick you and Michelle up. Do you want to go?"

Brad shrugged. "Yeah, sounds fun. I heard they're having pizza and playing games tonight."

"Great. I'm going to pick up Michelle now. She told me today she wanted to go too. You'll have to be ready in forty-five minutes. Go down and tell your dad."

She grabbed her purse and was out the door before Brad had even made it to the basement door. Good thing Brad wanted to go. If the kids wanted it, Chris had to agree, right?

Fifteen minutes later, she walked back into the house with Michelle by her side.

"Go upstairs and change your clothes. Jason's mom will be here soon."

As Michelle bounded up the stairs, Amy looked around for Chris, but he was nowhere to be seen. She found Brad wolfing down a bag of potato chips in the kitchen.

"You're going to be fed at youth group, you know. And I'd like you to go change. Put your new jeans on. Where's Dad? Did you tell him you're going to youth group?"

Brad mumbled through a mouthful of chips as he passed her on the way upstairs. "Yep. I told him. He's in the basement."

She stood in the kitchen, arms crossed, considering. Just then, she heard her husband coming up the stairs.

The door opened, and he stood there glowering. "Really?"

"Do you want to talk about it?" She knew he'd react this way, and she had a good argument prepared.

"No." He turned around and headed back down the stairs.

She rolled her eyes and sighed loudly. She went outside to wait for Pam—a little front porch rocker time was just what she needed now.

March 22

Jim started his day by spending time with God, then decided to call Chris in the hospital and hopefully cheer him up. He listened as Chris shared about his saga and was encouraged that his friend had been using some of the time thinking about their Bible study.

"I've asked God to help me figure out how my false identity of performance plays out in my relationship with Amy. When she criticizes me, I think I react in anger because I feel my performance is being questioned. She is often right about what she says, even if her delivery isn't the best. But my immature response to her starts our crazy pattern of arguing."

Jim was so surprised it took him a second to respond. "That's great, buddy. You're definitely on the right path."

"Thanks. I've learned a lot by considering my shortcomings as a husband and a Christian. Who knew I could learn so much from my faults? A real wake-up call for me. I've never bothered to examine my life in detail like this."

"It's worth it. No one wants to dig through painful stuff, but when we get to the root of the problem, there is hope for change."

"I realized another thing today. I want to be in control, and I've spent my life thinking I was. Everything seemed to go *my way*, according to *my plans*. Yet here I am, completely unable to control anything. This wasn't in my plans. Do you think God is trying to tell me something?"

"For sure. What do you think it might be?"

"Well ... for one thing, I'm not in control now. And yet, so far at least, I'm doing okay, and there's a lot to be grateful for. I think God is asking me to let him be in control of my life."

"That sounds like something God would ask of you. We either try to control our lives, or we let him be in control. Two people can't be in the driver's seat. It's very freeing to let God take the wheel. But we often want to be backseat drivers, so it will take practice to let go. I'll be praying for you to learn how to be a humble follower, asking for God's help and guidance, then obeying him. That will certainly bring you peace."

Chris rolled over to stop the spasm that was beginning in his back. "It would be great to feel peace, but I still want to take the wheel."

Jim chuckled. "I can relate. So do I. It's great to know what God is bringing to your mind. What will you do with that knowledge? For instance, how does that relate to your marriage?"

"When Amy tries to influence my spiritual path, it feels as if she wants to control me, and I balk. It's like a knee-jerk reaction. I resist because my faith is an intimate part of my life that I haven't shared with her. I feel like she thinks her faith practices are best. Feeling controlled hasn't led to vulnerability."

"I get that," Jim said. "So do you intend to share this with Amy?"

"Yes, but I want to do it face-to-face, rather than from a hospital bed. I bet if I looked up the word 'vulnerable' in the dictionary there would be an illustration of a person lying in a hospital bed."

Jim bellowed out a hearty laugh.

When it subsided, Chris yawned loudly. "Sorry. As much as I'm enjoying this, I'm getting really sleepy."

"I'll let you go. It was great talking with you. We'll talk again soon."

Chris dozed after Jim's call but was awakened by a sharp knock on his door. A short, wiry woman poked her head in, calling out, "Time to check your vitals again."

His eyes followed her quick hands efficiently pushing buttons, punching data into the keyboard, listening to his heart, and turning her cart around to leave.

"Everything looks fine and has been consistent. That's important if you want to get this surgery over with and get out of here."

Talking to Jim had been refreshing this morning. As much as Chris hated to admit it, his control issues were partly to blame for troubles in his marriage. He and Amy both wanted to be right all the time, even on things that didn't matter. And the control issues were tearing them apart. *Hadn't Jim once said selfishness and stubbornness were killers in marriage?*

Chris took advantage of the lull and said a small prayer.

God, I confess that I've resisted even good suggestions from Amy because I want to be in control.

Just then, a muscular Latino man in scrubs entered his room. His jovial voice bellowed through his mask. "Hey, my man, how are you doing?"

"Hey, Ray. You've been busy today. I haven't seen you much."

"I've been around. I see in the computer that you've been stable. I'm here to move you and say goodbye. The hospital is shifting things around. Our patients in this ICU are being moved to another one on the fifth floor so they can convert this one to a pandemic isolation unit."

"Wow, I guess that means they ran out of room in the first pandemic ICU? Will you have to take care of pandemic patients now?"

"Yes, I will." Ray held the thermometer near his forehead. "We've been getting extra training today in preparation."

"Are you worried about getting infected?"

"No, I'm young and healthy. I don't have any preexisting conditions." Ray wrapped the blood pressure cuff around Chris's arm, and it inflated automatically. "However, my dad lives with us, and I have small children, so I have to be incredibly careful."

"That's a lot to deal with, Ray. Thank you for all you do."

"You're welcome, man. Now let's get your stuff and find your new digs."

Once Chris was settled into his new room, he called Amy. He wanted to hear her voice.

She sounded breathless when she answered. "Are you okay?"

"Yes, I'm fine. I just called to give you an update. It's been a relatively good day—for a day in a hospital. My pain is under control. I got moved to a new ICU. The old one was converted to take on the extra pandemic patients. My new room number is 5014. This room isn't as new as the last one."

"Seriously? The pandemic patients are increasing?"

"Yeah. So, whatever they want to do to keep me away from the virus is fine with me. On another topic, I've heard the song 'Here Comes the Sun' a few times this morning on the public address system. My nurse said every time a patient comes off a ventilator, they play that song. It's encouraging, like when they play the lullaby song after a baby is born."

"That's a nice way to support those patients and the nurses as well. I've been wondering how you are doing. This is a lot to deal with. Are you afraid?"

He didn't hesitate. "Not at all, I feel amazingly calm."

Amy was silent for a moment.

He wondered if he had been convincing enough. "I can't explain *why* I feel so calm. Maybe it's a God-thing. How about you, are you afraid?"

"Yes," she said. "I'll admit it. I'm afraid enough for us both."

He yearned to comfort her. "I wish we could be together. I would give you a big bear hug."

"That would be so amazing."

"I love you."

"Love you too—more than you know."

After their call ended, Chris realized he hadn't considered her question beforehand. It didn't make sense, but he really wasn't afraid of dying. *Is it the meds? Or is it simply that I feel secure in my faith? I know—I truly know—I would be in heaven an instant after dying. How sweet would that be?*

He tapped his chin. *Should I call Amy back to let her know, or would she think I was being selfish?* He could imagine her saying, "Sure, you'll be in heaven, but I'll be left here picking up the pieces and trying to make do." He shook his head. *Better not to go there. Maybe God has more for me to do here anyway. Like telling Amy I have been at fault in our marriage and I plan to make changes.*

There it was—the reason he did not want to call her back. *I can be open with God and with Jim, but why is it so hard to be authentic and vulnerable with my own wife? When we decided to be all in for God at the marriage retreat, we were so open with each other. Now there's a wall between us.*

Chris wanted more time to work out how to talk to Amy about spiritual matters. He figured he had plenty of time. At least, he hoped so.

His thoughts turned darker. *There is also a risk I survive, but I'm left with significant disabilities.* Shivers crept down his spine at *that* possibility.

When Love Became a Cord of Three—Eight Years Ago

Chris whistled as he set some logs in the fireplace of their lanai. Jon and Jackie were on their way for a long-awaited reunion. The bond he felt for Jon had remained strong despite the busy years of becoming dads, developing careers, and doing life. He was glad his friends were moving back to Michigan, and he was looking forward to catching up on the years they lived away.

When his friends finally arrived, they all picked up right where they left off with friendly banter and reminiscing. After an hour-long chat over drinks, they sat down to a gourmet meal.

Jackie closed her eyes after chewing her last bite. "Amy, that lobster was wonderful."

"I have to give the credit to Chris. He ordered it to be flown in from Maine, and he cooked it. I made the squid ink pasta, though."

"I'm impressed." Jon raised his eyebrows. "You've managed to domesticate this guy."

"He's been a good sport about it. We love cooking together."

After that compliment, Chris felt obliged to help Amy clear the table. "I'm going to put coffee on. Let's sit on the lanai for dessert—go ahead out there. I'll light a fire in the fireplace in a minute."

When he brought coffee out, and Amy followed with cheesecake, Jon and Jackie were already curled up on the love seat with warm throws over their legs. The autumn wind was calm, but Chris made a fire anyway, then he and Amy sat opposite their friends in armchairs with throws tucked in around their legs too.

"Wow, this is so nice and cozy," Jackie said, snuggling up to Jon. "You would never know it's almost winter."

Amy said, "I guess that's one thing you'll have to adjust to in Michigan. Our winters are a *bit* harsher than Ohio's."

They all laughed.

Amy waved toward the house. "As the twins grew, we needed more space in our small house. We added a second story with new bedrooms and baths. We expanded the old bedrooms into a large family room and added this lanai."

Chris added, "Now we can spend more time outside when the weather cools off, and it's a great place to hang out with friends."

"We'll have to have you both over soon. We'll be living only a mile away." Jon pulled out his phone to show them pictures of their new place.

After Chris and Amy both commented on how nice their new house was, Jon took his phone back and said, "We'll close in five weeks. We can't wait to get out of the small apartment we rented. We're settling in, and we've already found a great church. Hey, you should go with us sometime."

Chris shrugged. "Maybe. We've been so busy with the twins' soccer games. They're often on Sunday. And work has been a killer lately. I just want to rest on the weekends. Amy usually goes to church without me now."

"No problem. We also signed up for a marriage retreat in Detroit in November. You should consider coming with us."

Jackie set down her dessert plate and pulled a brochure out of her purse, handing it to Amy. "It's nice because it's local. Would your parents come to watch the twins?"

Amy balanced her plate on her lap and took the brochure. "I think they would. This sounds like fun, especially if we get to go with you. What do you think?" She turned to Chris, holding the brochure out to him.

Who wants to have their marriage put under a microscope? Especially in front of their best friend. "Hmm. What's a marriage retreat like?" Chris said, without reaching for the brochure. He shoveled a big forkful of cheesecake into his mouth.

Jon leaned forward. "They have speakers and great music. Meals are on your own. Each couple gets a workbook to keep notes. And each night, the couples have some questions they can discuss in private."

Jackie added, "It's a great way to invest in your marriage. Our lives are so busy, we can easily forget to invest in us. Jon and I have gone to several different marriage retreats for that reason."

Chris finished chewing his dessert. *Maybe this will help us. Our marriage has been rough around the edges lately.* "Well, I'll go if you're up for it, Amy."

She raised her arms up in a V. "Yes!"

He was startled at her enthusiastic reaction. He quickly looked around to see everyone grinning, and he smiled in return. "I get the sneaking suspicion you and Jackie have been cooking this up all along." *Maybe she's as frustrated as I am.*

Jon waved his fork. "You won't regret it. Promise."

How can Jon be that gung-ho about it to go multiple times? That makes me curious. Chris nodded, then changed the subject to talk about work—a topic he was more comfortable with.

A few months later at the marriage retreat, Chris fidgeted with the program in his hand. He hoped he wasn't going to be put on the spot this weekend. He looked around at the large hall full of couples. He sat next to Jon, who seemed completely relaxed. Of course, Amy was happy. She probably needed a break from their conflict at home.

The crowd hushed as the curtains in front of the room swung open to reveal an empty stage except for two chairs facing each other. A distinguished older man hobbled onto the stage and sat in one chair. Then a young man entered the stage from the other side and sat in the chair facing the old man.

The older man said, "Tell me your life plans, son."

The young man said, "I'm going to graduate from the best university, so I can get a really good job."

The old man said, "And then what?"

"Well, I will work very hard to be quite successful."

"And then what?"

The young man listed accomplishments such as earning a lot of money, buying nice things, getting married, having a family, going on great vacations, and retiring to the South of France.

After each one, the old man asked, "And then what?"

When he ran out of accomplishments and dreams, the young man scratched his head. "Then I will be dead."

The old man leaned forward. "And then what?"

The young man's brow furrowed, and he shook his head. "I don't know."

The men sat, silently looking at one another for a full minute. It was so quiet in the auditorium, Chris wondered if Jon could hear his heart pounding.

The older man finally turned to the audience. "That's the *first* question we will answer on this retreat in order to get to God's plan for marriage." He turned to his younger companion. "Thank you, Rob."

People clapped as the young man left the stage, but the skit left Chris feeling unsettled. He'd never thought about death. Or that all his accomplishments would just end. As the old man went on to explain how everything in life was meaningless if Jesus was not the focus and center of their lives, Chris felt his heart beating fast. When the old man looked out into the sea of people, it was as if he were talking directly to Chris. He looked at Amy, and she was rubbing the back of her neck. *Is she thinking what I'm thinking?*

At the next break, he had a chance to talk to his wife. They stood in a quiet corner of the hallway, and he put his hand on her arm and looked deeply into her eyes. "Are you thinking the same thing I am? Why are we here? What's the purpose of our lives? I never realized how small my goals were. Or how nothing will be truly fulfilling and satisfying except a personal relationship with Christ. Have we been missing the point, thinking this life is all about us and our happiness?"

She nodded. "I couldn't have said it better. I'm glad we're here with Jon and Jackie. I feel comfortable asking them these questions. Do you?"

"Yes, I do. But right now, we gotta get back for the next session. I don't want to miss a single minute of this."

From time to time during the afternoon session, Chris glanced at Amy to see her reactions. He often caught a tear or a sniffle. It was all he could do to avoid crying himself.

He couldn't wait for evening to come so he could ask Jon and Jackie all the questions swirling around in his head.

Later, after picking up carryout, the four friends sat in their hotel room munching on the food and talking long into the night. Jon and Jackie openly shared their own faith journey and how it impacted their marriage. Chris and Amy were equally open, sharing how they had tried to do things their way and were left feeling empty and unfulfilled.

By two o'clock in the morning, Chris had all his questions answered. Jon showed him a prayer in the workbook they could use to ask God for a new start. Chris took Amy's hand and kneeled with her while Jon and Jackie stood and put their hands on their friends' shoulders.

Chris held the workbook and read the prayer out loud. "Dear Father, we have been trying to do life our way, and as a result, our lives are empty and unfulfilled. We want to change and do things your way. Thank you that Jesus died on the cross for us so we could have a personal relationship with you. We want that relationship and to give him complete control of our lives and marriage. Please send your Holy Spirit to be with us and make us into the people you want us to be. In Jesus's name, amen."

The group embraced and then wiped away their tears.

Chris realized then that even though they had been married in a church, they had never planned for God to be part of their marriage. But God had plenty of plans for him and Amy. God wanted them both to be in relationship with his Son, Jesus. Now the marriage lessons had more meaning and context. At the conclusion of the retreat, Chris and Amy stood with other married couples to renew their vows and promise to make a new start. The officiant then read from Ecclesiastes 4:9–12.

Afterward, Chris turned to Jon. "This time when that Scripture was read, I was struck by the last part about how 'a cord of three strands is not quickly broken.' I know you read this at our wedding, but it went right over my head. Is the third strand God?"

Jon smirked. "To quote my favorite Yooper, in terms he would best understand, *you betcha*."

"Touché," Chris said as they all enjoyed a belly laugh.

Later, when they drove home from the retreat, Chris glanced over at Amy. "I feel like we need to get active in church again. I want to be all in. What do you think?"

She beamed. "That's a great idea. It feels like we can have a fresh start now. I want to be all in too. We've just made a commitment in front of Jon and Jackie, who will hold us accountable. We have a chance to build a new legacy into the twins' lives by setting a different example."

March 23. Early Morning

Amy had been up and dressed since the crack of dawn for Chris's surgery. She found a large tote bag and carefully packed the items she had assembled—a phone charger, a card for Chris, printed emails from family and friends, photos of the family, a book, her ever-ready notebook and pen, snacks, and a couple bottles of water.

The short drive to the hospital brought back memories from three days ago when she raced to get him to the ER. Only this time, she didn't have any close calls with pedestrians. *Was that only three days ago?* As she approached the door, she noticed stanchions with yellow tape and large rectangle tables blocking the way just beyond the exterior doors.

As she stepped inside, a masked woman addressed her. "Ma'am, do you have a mask?"

The masks Yo had brought her were still sitting on the kitchen table. "No, I'm sorry I don't have one." She was embarrassed since there was a shortage of masks already.

The receptionist produced a mask and asked her to sanitize her hands. Then she asked why Amy was here.

"My husband is having surgery today, and they said I could come into the hospital to be with him."

"Your name please?"

"McGrath, Amy McGrath."

"Yes, I see you are on our list. Have you experienced a fever or chills in the past two days?"

"No."

"Any shortness of breath, cough, or difficulty breathing?"

"No."

"How about any fatigue, muscle or body aches, sore throat?"

"No."

She was sure she had heard these questions before. *Oh yes, it was when I dropped him off at the ER doors.*

"May I take your temperature?"

"Yes, it's fine."

The receptionist leaned forward across the table barrier and waved a thermometer at her forehead. "Okay, you're good to go. You can take this hallway to the elevators on the left. Your husband is in room 5014 on the fifth floor. I will let the nurses' station know you are on your way. Have a good day."

Amy received a "Well Visitor" sticker which she stuck to her jacket then headed down the long hall toward the elevators. The medical personnel were all gowned, masked, and gloved. Chris was right, this did remind her of the pandemic movie they saw years ago. She gingerly touched the elevator call button, feeling exposed without gloves on. *Maybe I should have taken this more seriously.*

To his surprise, Chris had a relatively good night's sleep, unlike the past two nights. He could hardly wait to see his wife. When would Amy get here? Would she be glad to see him? *I've been such a jerk lately. Where would I be without Amy?*

When she walked into his room, she tore off her mask and gave him a huge smile that lit up her beautiful hazel eyes. She dropped the bag she was carrying and wrapped him in a warm embrace.

Chris murmured in her ear, "Wow, you're a sight for sore eyes." *I almost forgot how gorgeous she is, just like the day I met her.*

She put her head down on his chest, and he heard her sob a little.

His eyes were wet too, and he clung to her as relief flooded through him. *We're together again.* He took her head in his hands and guided her toward him for a kiss.

He was reminded of how sweet their first kiss had been on the beach. It had been late in the evening, and they were alone, the dying embers of a bonfire still warming their bare toes. Chris had pulled Amy close, and she had leaned into him. He was barely breathing. His lips had met hers in a soft kiss while his hand had stroked her cheek. As he had drawn away, she had laid her head on his broad shoulder. They had watched the fireflies on the beach as the last embers of the fire died away.

When she stood up now, he could see their separation had been hard on her. Her face looked drawn, and her eyelids were puffy. Each of them looked away. He wanted to say something, but he couldn't get it out. She didn't speak either.

They had been sparring so much in the past few days, sometimes Chris wondered if she would even be there when he returned home.

He reached out for her hand, then squeezed it. "I'm glad you're here."

She blinked, squeezing his hand back. "I'm so thankful they let me come. I really wanted to be with you today, and I'd love to stay if they let me. Maybe I can hide out in a closet." Amy grinned.

Chris couldn't believe how relieved he felt just holding his wife in his arms. Their time apart had kindled a longing for her that he hadn't felt in the last few years. He cherished this woman and wanted her to know it.

"I'm sorry I've been so snarky lately." He decided now was the best time to make amends. What if he lost the ability to speak after today's surgery? Who knew how long they had left together? "Being alone made me realize how I've taken you for granted. There's no one I'd rather be with right now than you."

"I know you haven't been feeling well, and I was hard on you too."

That wasn't so hard. Her words warmed his heart, thankful they could come back to this place in their marriage. If he made it through this ordeal, he'd do better as a husband.

"How are you feeling today? Any headaches?" Amy gently stroked his head.

"I feel fine. The headaches have been controlled by medication since the second day I was here. The care is exceptionally good. Not having a roommate is nice. But I'm bored, and I just want to go home."

She smiled, then turned to the bag she'd brought. "I have some things that might help." She began unpacking gifts for him. Emails from friends and family members that brought tears to his eyes, photos which Amy taped up on the wall so he could see them and get-well cards which he read.

Then Amy brought her phone to him, and they took a couple of selfies together to send to their family. He tried his best to look normal in each one, but he could see his own drawn features in the camera. Everyone wanted to know the news, and soon her phone was blowing up with one text after the other responding to the selfie they'd sent.

"So many people are praying for you," Amy said as she scrolled through the responses and typed quick replies.

"Jim and Linda have organized a prayer team. Everyone is as shocked as we are. They all want to know how they can help."

"That's nice of them. I talked to Jim—he called me yesterday. I think it was a good idea for us to get mentors."

She looked up from her phone with wide eyes. "I think it's a good thing we have mentors too. I'm beginning to see how important they are to us." She paused, smiled, and said, "Speaking of the prayer team, do you think we should pray before your surgery? They may be coming in at any time to take you."

"I guess we could. I'm not comfortable praying out loud. But ... I'd like to."

"Me either, but this is important." She came over and clasped his hands. "It's just us. It doesn't have to be fancy."

He nodded. "Okay, I'll start." If she went first, she would say everything there was to say and then he'd have nothing left to say but "Yeah, what she said."

They bowed their heads, and Chris began.

"God, today Dr. Matthews is going to work his magic inside my skull to make me better. Please help him do an excellent job ..." He paused so Amy would realize he was done.

"Yeah, what he said. Amen."

Chris squeezed her hand and opened his eyes. Amy sat on the edge of his bed as they kept their hands clasped together. They chatted about mundane things, and their time together went by swiftly. Soon it was time for the surgery to begin. An orderly came in and began unplugging Chris from monitors, then wheeled him into the pre-op room. They allowed Amy to tag along. She walked by the side of his bed. After they positioned him in a curtained cubby, she stood by his side, with her hand on his shoulder. The slight pressure of her touch reassured him. *She is here for me. We're going to be okay.*

Finally, Chris saw Dr. Matthews enter the room, his smiling blue eyes visible above his face mask. Chris shook his hand, then introduced him to Amy. Dr. Matthews patiently went over the details of the surgery again, asking if either of them had any questions. They didn't.

"I came by your room earlier and saw you two praying, so I thought it might be okay if I prayed as well before we head down the hall."

Chris reached for Amy's hand, grateful for the faith of his doctor. "Go right ahead, Doc, that would be great."

Dr. Matthews bowed his head and prayed a simple prayer for God's blessing on the surgery. Chris struggled to hold back tears, while Amy openly swiped at her eyes with her free hand. When the doctor finished, the nurse gave Amy directions to the waiting room where she could pass the time.

Before Amy left, she gave Chris a big hug and a kiss. "I love you. He is a great doctor—everyone keeps telling me so. Before long, you are going to be home and better than ever. Can't wait."

"Me too." Chris watched her pull her mask back up and leave, turning once to wave at him. He felt a powerful ache in his heart. What would happen to him? To them?

The nurse patted Chris's shoulder and told him to relax, then a thick darkness engulfed him.

March 23. Early Afternoon

Amy trudged to the surgical waiting room, the long, empty hallway echoing her footsteps. With each step, a flood of worry threatened to overcome her. She turned the corner and stopped short. Before her was a large, silent room filled with empty beige chairs. She slowly panned the room with its green walls and dark carpeting. It shook her to realize she was the only one in here.

She collapsed into one of the chairs, then the worry swept in. She'd held it inside all morning so she wouldn't scare Chris, but now she could finally let go. She imagined the worst and fear overwhelmed her. *What if he can't talk or move part of his body when he comes out of this? How much care is he going to need when he comes home? What if the doctor is wrong, and he doesn't fully recover? What if he gets the virus? Will I be able to handle this?*

She got up and paced the room. It felt good to move, even if she was confined to this joyless room. She started feeling a little better. Chris's words came back to her. "Being alone made me realize how I've taken you for granted." Those words were much more precious than a bouquet of flowers.

I've taken him for granted too. Maybe there's a silver lining in this horrible experience. He'd said there was no one he'd rather be with than her. She pictured his tear-filled eyes holding her gaze, those eyes the color of hot chocolate with marshmallows stirred in. They still had the power to make her melt and go weak in the knees. *He does love me, after all.*

When the worrisome thoughts had run their course, she felt drained. She settled down in one of the chairs. There were hours of waiting ahead of her, and she was already starving, so she dug a water bottle and granola bar from her bag. Sleep seemed out of the question even though she was weary.

Her phone dinged with a text from Linda.

LINDA: How ya doing? I bet it was good to see Chris.

AMY: Sure was. Felt so good. I really love my husband!

LINDA: Never doubted it. How long do you think it will be?

AMY: They said four hours. There's no one here but me in a huge empty waiting room.

LINDA: So weird. Do you need anything? You know I clean when I'm stressed, and my house is already clean.

Amy rolled her eyes and shook her head.

AMY: Not that I can think of. Just pray!

LINDA: We all are! And we won't stop. I'm here if you need me.

AMY: Thank you. I'll let you know when he's out.

Three hours later, after eating two granola bars, pacing around the room, and taking a couple of trips to the bathroom, Amy pulled off her mask and curled up across three chairs to rest. *I'll just close my eyes for a second.*

She was awakened from a murky dream by the sound of footsteps coming toward her. Startled, she opened her eyes and realized Dr. Matthews was approaching. She looked up at the clock and saw she'd slept for over an hour.

She sat up, grabbed her mask, and hooked it over her ears. "Hi. Sorry, I guess I must have nodded off."

"No problem at all." He sat down a respectful six feet away wearing a mask. He had his surgery scrubs on, and she was glad to see there were no blood stains on them.

She held her breath as he spoke.

"The surgery went as planned with no concerns. He is still in post-op. When he's back in his room, someone will come and get you. You should be able to stay for about an hour with him. We are letting him wake up slowly, so it might be a while before you get to see him."

She slowly let her breath out in relief.

"We found an exceptionally large hematoma. Just as we expected, it was old blood. Kind of a jelly-like consistency. As we evacuated it, we could see the brain begin to puff back up a little. That's exactly what we wanted to see. We didn't see any indication of a current active bleed. We believe it had resolved itself.

"Mr. McGrath will have a drain in for a couple of days to let more fluid out. That will help the brain recover. He might have some trouble talking or moving his right side at first, so don't be alarmed if you notice that."

His news confused her. "The right side?"

"Yes. Remember, the left side of the brain—which we operated on—controls the right side of the body. So, he may lose motor skills on the right side of his body temporarily."

"Oh, yes." She thought about that. "Good thing he's left-handed."

"Also, the left side of the brain controls a lot of mental functions. If he has trouble talking, reasoning, or remembering, encourage him that he will improve over time. I will do the same. This usually resolves itself in the healing process. It could take up to a year. But we don't anticipate any long-term complications."

"Thank you, Doctor. We've heard wonderful things about you. We're glad you were available to do the surgery. When might he be able to come home?"

"It depends on how he does. We will want the drain out for at least a day before we send him home. But I think it might be reasonable to expect he could go home in five to six days."

"That sounds wonderful." She lifted her hand. "Oh, I almost forgot, one more thing. You mentioned a hematoma could be caused by taking baby aspirin. Do you think that was the cause?"

"It is hard to say. Why do you ask?"

She cringed. "Because I suggested he should be taking baby aspirin every day since his family has a history of heart attacks."

"Well, I wouldn't worry about that. According to my PA, Chris said his mom was the one who recommended it."

As the doctor headed out of the waiting room, Amy picked up her notebook and started writing. She paused with her pen in midair to relish a real sense of gratitude for the first time in a long time. It wasn't just thankfulness for a successful surgery. It was a deep sense of peace. God had answered their prayers. She also felt a deep and powerful affection for Chris. Earlier, she had texted *I really love my husband* to Linda. The text was a revelation—the love had been there all along but had been buried beneath layers of resentment.

Finally, a nurse came and brought Amy to Chris's room. He was sleeping soundly so she sat and watched him.

The doctor had evacuated the huge mass of blood from Chris's skull, but Amy felt like the huge mass of anger had also been evacuated from her heart. She felt free again, unburdened. *Thank you, God.*

Chris's eyes fluttered open, but then shut quickly from the blinding light above him. He tentatively opened one eye and saw Amy sitting in a chair next to his bed. He closed his eyes again and tried to remember what happened.

I'm in a hospital. My head hurts. Head ... oh, I had brain surgery. I'm awake and Amy's here, so it must be over.

After confirming he could wiggle his fingers and toes, he opened his eyes again and focused on his wife's beautiful face.

"Hey. Welcome back." Her soft words sounded like home.

He tried to lift his left hand to feel the bandage on his head, but she gently took his hand and kissed it.

"Are you in pain? The doctor said it could hurt to talk and eat for a while. The incision goes through the muscle which moves your jaw. Do you want to see the bandage?"

Chris nodded slowly. He felt as if he might undo all the surgeon's hard work if he moved too quickly.

Amy took out her cell phone and snapped a photo of his head, then held up the image for Chris to see. A huge swath of bandage curled around his head and a tube jutted out just above his forehead.

He cleared his throat, which felt scratchy. "Wow. Looks huge."

She gasped. "Oh, you can speak! Thank God." She grasped his hand and smiled down at him.

"What will the scar look like?" he asked.

"The scar won't be as noticeable after it's healed, but you're going to have some bragging rights."

He watched as her face lit up brighter than the room and heard a new tenderness in her voice. She kept touching him gently, running her hand over his shoulder and down his arm. He remembered the early part of their marriage before frustration and despair had crept in. When she had relished being near him and touching him. He enjoyed feeling like they were close again.

She began talking rapidly, rattling off the details. "Dr. Matthews said the surgery itself went fine. When anyone asked me who your surgeon was going to be, they raved about Dr. Matthews and his amazing bedside manner. What a blessing, given we had no say in the matter. I can't help but think we are going to see an end to this nightmare." She looked into his eyes and squeezed his hand between hers. "Not just the headaches, but the hard times between us. I feel like something new is happening."

Chris felt a wave of emotion at her words, and his eyes filled with tears. He squeezed her hand. "I do too."

"Life seems so full of promise now. Headaches should be gone. It wasn't a tumor or cancer. It was 'one and done.' I can't wait until you get home. Thank you, God, for answering our prayers." She smiled brightly and leaned in to peck him on the cheek.

He built up the courage to ask the question he most dreaded. "What's my recovery going to look like?"

She sobered as she sat back down on the chair. "The nurse gave me some information to read. Since you can talk already and you remember a lot, I'm very hopeful. But there might be times you will struggle with memory, attention, finding words, solving problems—things like that. Those are functions of the left side of the brain. But those will resolve in time. Also, the left side of the brain controls the right side of the body, so don't be surprised if you have some difficulty moving your right side."

He lifted his right leg and wiggled his toes under the sheet. "I don't like it that I might not think clearly. But I can move my right arm and leg, so that's good. Standing up and walking will be tested later, I guess."

She patted his shoulder. "Just relax. You just woke up. You'll start physical therapy in the next few days to determine what they need to help you with. But remember—I will be with you every step of the way. I'll help you. We'll get through this together." Her voice choked up. "I love you."

Chris felt stunned at how quickly their relationship had changed. How she had truly changed. But he had changed too. "I love you too," he said. "I couldn't do this without you. Thank you for being here for me."

They sat in silence for a few minutes, as he savored their closeness and affirmed love. Amy texted the photo of his big bandage to the family. Their son, Brad, texted back a joke about his dad having an even bigger head, and they both laughed. More texts came in, and Chris enjoyed listening to her read them.

They spent two full hours together before she had to leave, and he was grateful it was a time of joy instead of the strife they'd most recently experienced as a married couple.

After Amy left, he looked around his room, feeling exhausted and drained. The day had grown dark outside, and he could see his reflection in the window glass. *I look gruesome. There's a huge bandage, a drain coming out of my forehead, an IV in my arm, and a catheter. But those things are temporary. I can finally relax. It's over.*

Amy said she loved me and would be with me every step of the way of my recovery. It's amazing how we've both recognized our love for each other through this scary time. As she said, new times are ahead for us.

Was it possible that things between them had miraculously changed? Would it be lasting?

Drowsiness set in, and he didn't try to resist it. It had been so long since he could sleep soundly without a headache. Now, he had no more fears he might have brain cancer. The hematoma had been removed without complications. Things just might be getting better between him and Amy.

Thank you, God, he silently prayed before he gave in to sleep.

March 24

Amy pulled out the onions and mushrooms she had sautéed a few nights before. She cracked two eggs into her frying pan and whisked them. Once they set, she sprinkled the vegetables on top of her omelet. As she cooked, she realized her old, constant aggravation with Chris was gone, replaced by an upbeat feeling. It was good to remember how they'd clung to each other and their faith before the surgery, then had such a wonderful bonding time after the danger was over.

After eating, she dressed. There was a list of practical things she could do which made her feel energized.

The phone rang, and she saw it was the hospital. She hoped it was Dr. Matthews with his report, so she grabbed her notebook.

"This is Dr. Matthews. I'm in your husband's room. Looks like he had a good night's sleep. He has some pain from the incision which cut part of the temporalis muscle, but it was expected. He says his pain's not bad, and the CT scan from this morning looks good. There is a little re-expansion of the brain, but we would like to see more."

Amy scribbled everything down in her notebook.

"There's only a tiny bit of oozing from the drain, and normally we see much more. We may have the PA adjust the drain. It will be boring for him because he must lay almost flat on his back until the drain comes out. Later, we might roll him on his left side so gravity can help the brain expand back to where it should be. We'll be watching for headaches, and each day we'll do another CT scan to monitor progress. Once his drain is out, he can be moved out of the ICU."

Amy continued scribbling notes as the doctor spoke. "All that sounds surprisingly good," she said when he paused. "I was grateful to hear him talk after the surgery. He sounded perfectly normal."

"Yes, I think so too. Sometimes a person who has had a craniotomy will have periods when things are a little off, but then the next day they might bounce back. It's normal. So don't be alarmed if you notice changes in his speech. I do these surgeries often, but they are usually on people much older than your husband. Plus, many of the patients have had some head trauma. But since the cause of the bleed is undetermined, we're being cautious and keeping a close eye on his recovery."

"Wow, recovery from this surgery sounds easier than I imagined. Who would have known? Thank you again, Dr. Matthews, for all you've done. We are both greatly relieved."

Amy ended the call then sat looking out the window. She noticed tiny buds popping out at the ends of tree branches even though the sky was gray and snow flurries were expected. Signs of spring were blossoming outside and in her heart.

The ringing of her phone again startled her. She picked it up and noticed Jon's name on her screen. "Hello, Jon. I guess you saw my email about Chris?"

"Hi. Yes, I just saw it this morning. The email address is an old one we don't often check. Sorry about that. I'll send you the best one for future emails."

"Oh, that's okay. I did wonder if the address I had was still valid, but I couldn't check with Chris. It's so good to hear your voice."

"Even better to hear yours. Can I add Jackie to the call?"

"Sure, great idea."

"Hey, girl. We're sitting here in shock about Chris. What is the latest, and how can we pray?"

Amy felt the surge of love from her friends through the phone boosting her optimism about Chris's recovery. "Well, I just hung up with his neurosurgeon. His surgery was yesterday. At this point, things look pretty encouraging for a full recovery after some rehab."

"Oh, that is a definite answer to prayer," Jon said. "Listen, I'm also sorry we speak less often since we moved back to Ohio. I really want to drive there to see him in person. What are the visitor rules in his hospital?"

"They won't let visitors in. I was only allowed in yesterday for the surgery."

"Oh no. I can't imagine what that must be like." Jon paused on the other end as Amy waited. "Well, please tell my roomie that I love him, and we're praying for him. Can I pray for you now?"

"Please."

"God, I ask you to give Amy peace and comfort as she waits for Chris to return. Please give her confidence that you have a plan for them that is good. Please give the doctors and nurses the focus and ability to do their part in his care. We ask for you to heal him and to give us patience and peace to accept your timing. Your will be done, in the name of Jesus."

"Amen," they said together.

Chris woke to the sounds of "Here Comes the Sun" coming through the public address system and took stock of his situation. *No headache. No pain unless I move my jaw. Can still move my fingers and toes.* Tiny snowflakes blew lazily by his window in the gray sky. Three nurses were visible behind the window to the hallway, leaning over the computer screen and talking. *Are they talking about me?*

Allie, who had been his nurse for a couple of days, looked up and waved at him, then came into his room. "Hi. How are you feeling?" She moved the vital signs monitor cart near him and punched in some data on the keyboard.

"I feel surprisingly good. But I really want to go home. When will the drain come out?"

Allie briefly pointed the non-contact thermometer at his forehead. "Probably not today. The CT scan they did last night showed your brain needs to expand further still. It's likely the drain will remain for a few more days. You'll have to stay in an ICU until then."

"*An* ICU? Why not *this* ICU? You're not kicking me out, are you?" He loved teasing Allie—she had a great sense of humor.

"It's not my choice, but yes, you must leave here. Unfortunately, the pandemic patients are still multiplying, and this unit will be converted for them."

"Wow, I hope you don't run out of ICUs."

She paused from wrapping the blood pressure cuff around his arm. ", your *new* ICU is being converted from a PACU. Do you know what that is?"

"No."

"It's a post-anesthesia care unit. Where patients go after surgery. We used to call them recovery rooms. You'll be the first patient to be moved there." She continued to tighten his cuff and soon it began to inflate. "We have to make some adjustments, and since we all like you so much we decided to let you be the guinea pig." Allie laughed.

"Great. Nothing I like better than to be a guinea pig. I hope at least I'll get filet mignon for helping you out."

Allie played along. "Yes, you will. Candles and flowers and a strolling violinist too."

Allie soon finished with his vitals, and it wasn't long before someone came to move his bed to the new unit. Chris watched the walls and hallways as he passed. *How many other beds containing pandemic patients have passed through these hallways?* His pending transfer to the PACU-ICU left him feeling anxious. His jaw tightened. Would he receive the same great care in a makeshift ICU? How would they ensure he would not be exposed to the virus?

After the patient transporter positioned his bed in the small, curtained cubby, his nurse propped him up on his side against a rolled-up blanket so gravity would assist the drain in his head. He would be stuck here until the drain was removed, which could not be rushed.

He heard all the conversations around him through the thin curtains as the nurses adjusted to their new setting. They were frustrated the PACU computers wouldn't dispense certain medications since normally the patients were only there to be weaned off anesthesia, and they needed to pass through the pandemic unit to get the medications they required. He overheard all sorts of scary-sounding questions from the staff when they didn't know he could hear. Then, one by one, he heard other patients being moved into the unit.

The hours dragged by, but Chris could not sleep or get comfortable even as the hour grew late.

A catheter in one end and a drain in the other kept him immobile, and he grew restless. His fretting had been on repeat for hours now. The same negative thoughts whirled around, gaining momentum like debris in a tornado. Any possibility of more sleep went sailing away.

God help me. When will this long night be over? His thoughts turned sour. *Every time I nod off to sleep, an alarm from the guy's equipment next to me wakes me up. The bright light feels like it's searing a new hole into my brain. They said it can't be dimmed. My back aches something fierce, and I'm not allowed to roll over. I can't even get out of bed by myself. Will the pandemic patients ever stop? What if the whole hospital fills up with them? Will I have to move into a tent outside the hospital? I need to get out of here.*

The alarm in the cubby next to him went off again, only louder and more insistent. He could hear several nurses come running. A flurry of activity ensued. He could only imagine what was happening. By the curt conversation between the nurses, he could guess the guy next door was in much worse condition than he was. His self-pity ground to a halt.

Wow, here I am grousing about feeling uncomfortable, and this poor guy next to me may be dying. Sounds like he's on a ventilator. I saw those images on TV. So much equipment you could barely see the person. How scary must that be? Is he even aware of what's happening to him? Maybe I can pray for him. I know lying here grumbling isn't making me feel any better.

He turned his thoughts away from his own suffering and asked God to help the man next to him. *God, will you help that man? I don't know his name, but I'm sure you do. He doesn't have any family here. He may not even know what's happening to him. Oh, and will you also help the nurses? They sound stressed. I know that one, Shirley, came out of retirement to help. I think she is a little overwhelmed. Thank you.*

The alarm stopped, and the nurses retreated. Quiet was restored, and soon Chris felt himself relaxing.

But his rest was short-lived. Alarms woke Chris again. He heard several people weeping behind the curtain. The man's family must have come. At first, he was jealous the man had visitors. But then he realized it was unlikely his neighbor even knew his family was there. Chris heard low murmurs, and then, the machine ceased beeping. The silence was punctuated by sobs. All he could feel was sadness for them.

Before long, the PA came to his bedside and fiddled with the position of the craniotomy drain. When he asked, she said they still had not collected enough fluid to remove the drain. His heart sank. *C'mon, God, I need to get out of here.*

March 25

Chris shifted his legs a little, trying to get comfortable. It didn't help. He fumbled with his phone for the umpteenth time, checking his email. Nothing. But at least it was seven o'clock. He thought Amy would be up by now, so he called her. She answered on the first ring.

As soon as she picked up, he launched into his get-it-done voice. "I need to get out of the PACU-ICU. I don't think I slept all night. There were horrible bright lights shining in my eyes. And the noise is disruptive. Curtains don't keep much out. I can hear what the nurses are saying, and the machines constantly beep. I need rest if I'm going to recover enough to go home. I don't know how much more of this I can take."

Amy spoke softly. "I'm sorry to hear that. You sound really frustrated. Do you still have the drain in?"

Chris quickly replied. "Yeah. I know what you're going to say. That the drain must be removed for me to leave the ICU. But I'm *desperate*."

Amy murmured, "Aww. Are you scheduled for another CT scan today?"

He took a deep breath, then said, "They usually do one early in the morning to see if anything has changed."

"Your nurse said the drain is putting out less fluid, so maybe the scan will show there is no need to keep the drain."

He turned his head a little to check the fluid level of the drain bag resting upon his pillow. "I'm no expert but it looks the same to me."

"Would you mind if I pray for you now?"

"That would be great. Be sure to ask for a miracle."

"Dear God, you know everything that is going on with Chris, and we pray for the drain to be removed."

"What she said, amen," Chris responded.

That afternoon, Dr. Matthews's PA came in and informed Chris that today's scan showed the drain could be removed. He was apprehensive about that ghastly-sounding procedure, but he knew it was his ticket out of this disruptive unit. Midway through the procedure, as two stitches were removed and the drain was pulled out without anesthesia, the pain gave him second thoughts, but he gritted his teeth and endured it.

Shortly after, his nurse came to share great news. "Looks like you'll be leaving us. Now that the drain is out, you'll go to a new floor. I'll miss you. It's rare for a patient to be praying for me, and I appreciate it."

Chris smiled the best he could. His incision was feeling better, but any facial movement still made him wince. "Where will they be taking me?"

"Let's see." She consulted her chart. "You'll be on the seventh floor, the oncology department, because that's a pandemic-free location. They should be coming for you soon." She turned from the computer screen and smiled. "Is there anything I can get you before you leave?"

"No, I don't think so. I appreciate all you've done in challenging times like this."

She patted his shoulder. "Patients like you make my job so much easier. Thank you."

"Caring for patients is definitely a mission for you. I remember a business seminar where the presenter stressed the difference between involvement and commitment. He said that in a bacon-and-egg breakfast, the chicken was *involved*, but the pig was *committed*. It isn't a perfect analogy, but you are a lot closer to commitment than simply involvement."

She chuckled. "I don't know if I like being the pig, but that's a great analogy."

A few minutes after the nurse left, a patient transporter came to wheel Chris in his bed to his new room. As they exited the elevator to the seventh floor, Chris noticed more upscale paintings and decorations. When they entered his room, he could hardly believe his eyes. This room was no tiny, curtained cubby without a TV. He imagined they must reserve this room for VIP's.

He called Amy as soon as he could. "You're never going to believe it, but I got the drain out and left the PACU-ICU. Guess where my new room is. It looks like a penthouse."

"Wow, that's awesome. Let's FaceTime. I want to see."

Switching to the rear facing camera, Chris panned the phone around the room for Amy to see. "Look at this huge window. I didn't have that in the makeshift ICU. It's so nice to see outside again. Did you know there's a golf course next to the hospital? I never realized that."

He continued to pan around the room from his bed. "There's room enough for a second bed, but I get to stay here alone. I also have a TV and look at how large it is. Now I won't be as bored. Can you see the bathroom? The tiles are upscale. And it's totally quiet here. I am at peace in this room. I think I could stay in the hospital longer if I got to stay here." He looked at her image in the corner of the phone, and she was laughing. "What do you think?"

"I think you're making me dizzy, but I'm thrilled to hear you sound like yourself again!"

"Oh, sorry—I didn't mean to wave it around so fast. Do you want me to show you again?"

"No, it looks amazing. But don't get too comfy there—I want you home. It could be as early as tomorrow, you know. Hey, flip the screen back to your face."

He switched the view. "I still look pretty scary, but I'm relieved to have that drain out."

Amy's eyes softened. "Man, are you ever a sight for sore eyes. I don't care how many bandages you have on. I can't wait to be able to hug you."

"Me too." He couldn't take his eyes off her. "Oh, trust me, I won't get too comfy here. I am dying to get home. Hey, I've been meaning to tell you something."

"What?"

"When they were getting ready to put me out on the operating table, I overheard Dr. Matthews use a four-letter word."

"Seriously? I'm surprised. He seems like such a conservative guy. What did he say?"

"Oops."

It took her a moment to realize he was joking. She laughed so hard she snorted. "You almost had me there."

"Gotcha. I love to make you laugh. It's been rough being apart all this time."

"Yes, I can hardly stand it … I really miss you."

"I miss you too. A lot."

She blew him a kiss, and he tried to pucker up. "Sorry, babe, it hurts my head. But I'll make it up to you later." He winked.

After they hung up, he basked in happiness. He could not recall how long it had been since he felt this relaxed, confident, and at peace.

He spent the rest of the day humming along to music on his phone.

March 26

The next day, Amy finally got the call she'd been waiting for—time for Chris to come home. When she arrived on the hospital grounds, there were signs everywhere she hadn't noticed when she came for the surgery. One exceptionally large hand-painted sign on the lawn read: WE LOVE MEDICAL WORKERS. In the hospital windows were signs from the medical personnel: WE'RE TAKING GOOD CARE OF YOUR LOVED ONES.

As she got in line with the other cars under the covered entrance, she saw someone unloading trays of food. She had heard about service groups donating food to the hospital personnel. She shook her head in amazement at how people had sprung into action to show compassion and concern for others. It made her feel good to live in this supportive community.

At last, it was her turn to pull up in front of the doors. She spotted Chris being pushed in a wheelchair toward her. Her heart pounded. The large bandage covering his incision was gone, and she could see the forty-two, sparkling stainless-steel staples that graced his half-shaved head and looked like a gigantic question mark from his forehead to his left ear. He was a sight to see. But he was *her* sight to see.

After the nurse settled him into the car, she gave Amy a packet of information. "These are instructions for his care at home and a list of doctors to call. They want to have him come back for a CT scan in about a week. Then in two weeks, you will see Dr. Matthews to remove the staples. If you have any questions, there is a number to call. Let us know if you need anything. Get well soon, Mr. McGrath." The nurse stepped back and waved as the car pulled out.

Amy pulled forward but stopped the car at the end of the drive. Turning to him, she took his head in her hands and kissed him tenderly.

Once they were home, she got him settled on the sofa in the family room, a drink of cold water by his side. There was a lot to do—medicine to pick up at the drugstore, things to put away, appointments to schedule, dinner to prepare. But right now, all she wanted to do was cuddle with her husband.

She snuggled up to him on the sofa. "It's wonderful to have you back home. It felt empty here without you."

"I can't imagine what it was like for you being all alone."

"It was a horrible thing for both of us. But we not only survived—we thrived. Our love kept us going."

He held on to her tightly. "I'll never stop loving you. We did thrive, that's a good way to put it. We have a lot to celebrate. Let's sit here for the rest of the night."

She laughed. "Well, we'll be hungry soon. We can't just sit here all night. But wow, it feels so good to have you back." She laid her head on his shoulder and they clung to each other.

After dinner, she arranged a video call with Linda and Jim to give them an update.

Jim spoke first. "How ya doing, buddy?"

"Pretty amazing for the third day after surgery."

"How did it feel to have a surgeon's hands inside your skull?"

Chris laughed. "Unlike some of the doctor shows you see on TV, I was not awake during the surgery. I was totally out. I remembered the surgeon praying for all of us right before surgery, and then my next memory was Amy's beautiful face."

Both Jim and Linda asked at the same time, "The surgeon *prayed* for you?"

Amy nodded. "Yes, he's a Christian."

Jim gave her a thumbs-up. "That's encouraging," he said.

Linda asked, "Are you able to walk?"

"Yes, but I'm a little wobbly. It might be due to how long I spent in bed, plus my brain is still recovering."

Jim leaned forward in his seat. "Let's see your scar."

Chris turned his head so their mentors could be impressed with the full effect of the ghastly incision. "Dr. Matthews said there are forty-two staples. Kinda looks like railroad ties for a Micro Machines toy train."

Linda grimaced. "Are you in any pain now?"

"Surprisingly, only minor pain if I lay on that side of my head—from the incision."

"I'm glad the mechanics of the surgery were not as horrible as I expected," Jim said. "How did you feel emotionally about the whole experience?"

Chris rubbed his chin. "Overall, I was surprised at how calm I was. But there were moments of pure panic. I must admit my gut churned several times at the beginning. It completely terrified me because I didn't know if it meant I was going to die. But when they explained the blood could be removed with a high success rate, I lost my fear. Then I had this unexplainable sense there was a definite purpose to what I was going through. I was supposed to be here, at this time, in this place, for some reason. I surprised myself at how chill I was. If that makes any sense."

Jim nodded. "That makes perfect sense. We all go through tough times, but if we look for the higher purpose, our perspective changes. It's like seeing the 'big picture' in business terms."

Chris looked up for a moment. "Isn't there some Scripture verse along the lines of counting it as joy when you face troubles so your endurance can grow? It was tough to go through everything. First, not knowing how the surgery would turn out, then being moved so many times, and the pandemic complicating everything. I think I did okay, but I don't know if I felt joy."

Jim said, "Joy is a choice, which doesn't come automatically or instantly. That verse is in the first chapter of James. God allows troubles to test our faith. If you trust that God will work something good out of them, that's what 'counting it as joy' means. In the long run, problems can make your endurance—or stamina—grow. After a while, you can approach difficult times knowing you'll find joy on the other side."

Chris didn't say more. He felt stirrings of deeper emotions about his marriage, but he wasn't ready to share them yet.

March 30. Morning

Faint birdsong reached Amy's ears before her eyes opened. The day already felt luxurious to wake up without panic or fear greeting her. The former anger that usually boiled beneath the surface of her marriage had passed. Three whole days with Chris home from the hospital had flown by without her feeling an ounce of contention. Things were good. She lay in bed for a few minutes, listening to the birds serenade her. Gradually, she became aware there were no sounds of breathing next to her. She rolled over and opened her eyes. Chris was gone. *I don't hear him in the bathroom. Where could he be?*

She bounded out of bed and slid into her slippers. After grabbing a robe, she rushed out of their bedroom. There were no lights on in the upstairs hall, and she heard nothing anywhere in the house.

Her throat tightened as she descended the stairs and flipped on lights in the dark house. What if he had fallen or something had happened in his brain? Her steps became quicker as she bounded off the last step.

"Chris?"

She rushed through the dining room and the kitchen. Finally, she noticed a light in the family room. She hurried in, relieved to see he wasn't on the floor or unconscious.

"Why are you up so early?"

He turned to her from his spot on the couch, tears rolling down his cheeks.

"What's wrong? Are you okay?" She joined him on the sofa and wrapped her arms around him.

Chris didn't speak for a moment, but then finally whispered, "I'm okay ... nothing wrong. I keep thinking how blessed I am. What if my PCP didn't have me do the 'drunk walk' last week? What would have happened to me if they hadn't sent me to the ER? Then the amazing Dr. Matthews was the one to do my surgery. What if someone else had done the surgery, and I ended up with serious complications? What if I caught the virus? It was spreading so quickly through the hospital." Chris paused to take in a deep breath. "I've been thinking of all the things that worked out for good. Here I am at home, doing well in my recovery, and I have hope for a good future."

By this time, she was getting weepy too. "I know. It's incredible and overwhelming. We are blessed things worked out the way they did."

Chris turned and pulled her closer, and she rested her head on his chest and wiped her eyes.

"But what gets to me more than anything ..." His voice faltered. "I could have died ... might never have seen you again ... might never have come home. And at a time when our relationship was in such a mess. When Jim asked me about emotions the other day, there was more I could have shared, but I wanted to do that with you privately first."

He held her tightly. "I had a lot of time to think when I was in the hospital. I'm so sorry for believing everything between us was your fault. I was blind to my own huge failures, but I see things differently now. It's positive, like a wall has been broken down, and the good feelings in me that were buried are finally able to come out, if that makes any sense."

She sat up and looked at him through her watery vision. "I was afraid you weren't coming back, and we would never get a chance to talk about us. I'm glad you shared this. It means the world to me. We can be better together. I've missed you, and I don't just mean in the last week. It's been a long time since we were emotionally connected. You're right, there was a wall between us ... and now it's gone. I forgive you."

They sat together on the sofa for the longest time, the sound of their sniffles accompanying the ticking of the clock.

When the pinks and oranges of the sunrise lit up the family room, Amy sat up. "I guess it's time for breakfast. Should I make your favorite?"

"Yes, ma'am. Bacon and eggs here I come."

After breakfast, Chris watched as Amy fussed about like a mother hen. She cleared the table and brought him a handful of pills to swallow.

Enjoying his wife's delicious meals and sound sleep next to the love of his life did wonders for his recovery. And he couldn't believe how great he felt to be headache *and* conflict free.

"Look, Chris." Amy waved a pile of pages she'd pulled off the printer. "You'll be proud of me. I made a spreadsheet to help me keep track of your meds, doctor visits, and therapy sessions."

He held his arms out to her. "Come here, beautiful." He pulled her to his lap and held her for a moment, relishing this renewed sense of closeness.

She gave his shoulders a squeeze. "Our church added a page to their website and challenged people to send videos of what they are doing to pass the time during the quarantine. Do you want to watch some now?"

"Sure." He sympathized with other people being sequestered inside their homes. Although they hadn't been through major brain surgery, he imagined they shared his sense of cabin fever.

He followed Amy to the family room. She picked up the remote and connected the TV to the church website. They settled down to watch. One video showed a family with young children jumping on a trampoline. Another showed an older couple putting a puzzle together. Another family was doing yoga. And a young couple showed off their dance skills.

When the videos ended, Chris turned to his wife. "Do you think we could do a video? I've never considered myself a good dancer, but I'm passable with slow dances. What if we danced to a slow song and at the end, we turn, and I reveal the scar on the side of my head? That would be a dramatic way to show what we've been up to."

Amy smiled. "I love that idea. Let's do it."

She found the tripod and a YouTube video of Mary Chapin Carpenter's version of "Grow Old Along with Me."

As they danced, he sang to the song, or at least he tried, since his voice was so weak only some of the words were audible. Choreographing their moves was difficult for Chris, but he patiently worked through the many video do-overs until they had it just right. Once they muscled through, they watched it together. Neither one of them could speak by the end when they turned around to reveal Chris's scar. Tears rolled down his cheeks.

After a long afternoon nap, Chris sat alone in the family room reading his notes from the Bible study he had been doing with Jim.

He was drawn to a section he had highlighted where the author talked about God shaping and crafting each person internally. How our unique personality, thoughts, dreams, temperament, feelings, talents, gifts, and desires made up an authentic "us."

Tears began to flow when he came to the next three pages. His false sense of identity—his inauthentic self—had reacted with anger and escape when Amy criticized him. Instead of hearing her suggestions to make himself better, he only heard, "You're not good enough." He had given into the temptation to believe this lie too many times. Shuddering, he considered the being who was behind such horrible distortions of the truth.

He closed his eyes in prayer. "God, I've been believing lies about who I am, and that has caused me to react to Amy by running away and avoiding her. I must admit, sometimes she was right, I did need to change. But I was so stuck in my false identity I couldn't hear the truth in her words. You paid the ultimate price for my freedom to be who you created me to be. From this day forward, I want to live authentically. I want to be able to accept loving correction on the path to grow to be more like you."

Chris immediately wanted to share his observations with Jim, who had been texting him off and on since the four of them spoke. The new, raw Chris had been reluctant to talk to anyone by himself since the surgery. Finally, he decided to jump in and call his mentor for a one-on-one chat. Of all the men Chris knew, Jim was the one he could be comfortable with being "the real Chris."

Jim's animated voice greeted him on the other end of the call. He told Chris Linda was making a meal for him and Amy, and Jim would it bring by this afternoon. He promised to leave it on their doorstep, ring the bell, and leave. This quarantine thing had already become tedious, but Jim said he didn't want to inadvertently expose them to the virus.

After Chris thanked him, he directed the conversation to what had been bothering him. "Jim, some unusual things have been happening. I'm thinking differently. I almost don't know where these thoughts are coming from."

"What do you mean?"

"It's hard to describe. I see things and hear things differently than before. No ... that's not right. It's that I *feel* things differently than before."

"Are you talking about side effects?"

"No, sorry, I mean I'm doing a lot of self-evaluation. I've been thinking a lot about our Bible study. I'm beginning to understand it better now."

"That's great. Which part?"

"The part about getting over my wall. I never saw the roadblocks in my life before. But now I know what the issues are that keep me from being the man God designed me to be."

"Yes, we all have them. They prevent us from living in our identity. Have you taken the next step?"

"Yes. I told God I was sorry for the lies I believed about myself."

"Such as?"

"That my old identity was defined by what I did, what I had, and what other people thought about me. I think I cannot be vulnerable with Amy because I might have to admit that relationships are more important than things and other people's opinions. I react badly when she says something that feels to me like she's trying to change me. I take it as a criticism when she may have intended it to be helpful. But my old identity wasn't what God wanted for me. Being in the hospital helped me give up control to God, so I could be the man he intended me to be."

"Did you discover your true identity?"

"Yes. My identity from God is being his son, through my faith in Jesus. It's about relationship—with him and others. Not achievements, material things, or what others think of me."

"Absolutely. I'm really impressed. You've taken a huge step that will affect the whole trajectory of your life. I can't wait to see how this new perspective will benefit your marriage."

Chris blew out a breath. "Me too. I finally surrendered, and now I feel like a new person. That's probably why love and gratitude keep bringing up so much emotion inside me. I only regret it took a freaking brain surgery to get me to do that."

Jim laughed. "A *freaking* brain surgery. That's good. I've heard it credited to Mark Twain that the two best days in a person's life are the day they are born and the day they discover why. Feels good to know your identity, doesn't it? And if it took a freaking brain surgery, then so be it."

Chris choked up. "Well said. I've broken through my self-imposed prison. I appreciate your help in my journey. I'm relieved you wouldn't let me say no to doing that Bible study with you."

"I had to push because I knew you'd be glad in the end. Even when you were snarky and told me you couldn't imagine how discussing ancient undecipherable words with another man could revamp anyone's thinking."

They both laughed.

"Boy, was I wrong. Thanks again for not giving up on me."

He heard a noise and turned to see Amy stomping away from the doorway.

March 30. Evening

Amy hadn't been eavesdropping on purpose. She had been straightening up the house and didn't know Chris was on the phone. She had walked into the room intending to ask him if he needed anything. When she realized he was on the phone, she'd stopped to wait and then realized he was talking with Jim. Chris had a familiar tone, as if they talked all the time. That was news to her since Chris hadn't told her he was still meeting with Jim. Her face lit up with an approving smile. She leaned on the doorframe, waiting for a break to ask Chris what he might need, since she wasn't in his line of vision. But she froze when she heard the next words out of his mouth.

"I'm relieved you wouldn't let me say no to doing that Bible study with you."

Thoughts slammed through her mind as she reeled with this new information.

Chris is doing a Bible study? With Jim? Seriously? She turned to go before Chris saw her but wondered if her feet had betrayed her as they slapped angry thoughts on the hard tile floor. She spent some time on the front porch, trying to rock her irritation away, but she ended up only feeling worse. The March air was cold, but she barely felt it over her hot rage. How could Chris have kept that from her? He knew she'd wanted to study the Bible with him but had refused many times. After a few moments, she began to feel her anger ebb. When her temper cooled to a slow simmer, and before she wore grooves into the porch decking, she got up to go inside.

She found Chris in the kitchen making a snack. She joined him in stony silence. Would he bring it up? Or would he just avoid the topic like he did with so many other things?

She grabbed a cracker even though she wasn't hungry. Chris put down the cheese spread and turned to face her. "I guess you overheard me talking to Jim. I was waiting for the right time to tell you what I've been learning about my relationship with God."

She stopped to listen, folding her arms across her chest.

"It's not easy for me to talk about this, but I owe it to you to try. I want to stop running away from conflict and work things out. Sometimes, I'll need a little time to get my act together, that's why I didn't come out to the porch right away. But I'm ready to share my perspective now. Is that okay?" Chris leaned against the counter and rubbed his jaw.

She was cautiously intrigued. Amy raised her eyebrows and nodded.

"I started doing a Bible study with Jim a while back, and it has impacted me quite a bit. He had done this study before, and he recommended we go through it together. I doubted I'd stick with it, which was why I didn't tell you then. But each week, I couldn't stop thinking about the questions, and I needed to talk with Jim about them. I kept going back to it even though it was challenging and uncomfortable."

Amy saw the sincerity in his eyes, but she still seethed because he'd kept this important news from her. She didn't say anything because she wanted to hear more.

He shifted uncomfortably, then sat down on a barstool. While sneaking glances at her, he drummed his fingers on the countertop and continued. "I've been on a hamster wheel for much of my life. I desperately wanted to avoid the financial failures of my parents. I started by rushing to finish college so I could begin making money. Then I pushed my career into overdrive so the kids could have the things I didn't have."

Finally, he turned to look at her fully. "Even though I make my motivations sound noble, I now know I was driven to prove myself. I thought my worth was in how much I made and how successful I was. I couldn't risk getting off the hamster wheel and seeing myself as a failure."

She leaned back against the counter. This was eye-opening and new to hear her husband reveal his secret thoughts. She had plenty to say but held her tongue.

"At the marriage retreat ten years ago, we decided to get serious about God. I didn't totally change but simply added God onto my growing list of responsibilities. I know I didn't balance all the priorities well, and that never stopped haunting me." Chris ran a hand over his jaw again, as if searching for the right words. "I did a great job of being a leader in the fullest sense of the word at work. Setting a vision and mission to charge off in new directions. But at home, I haven't even tried to engage in that kind of leadership. I haven't invested in relational things—our marriage or my faith. I was pushing too hard and working too much to even think about it. I felt like you never ..." He stopped and frowned.

She held still but didn't speak.

After blowing out a huge breath, Chris put up his hands in a defensive stance. "Don't get mad, okay? I'm trying to be honest here."

She nodded slowly.

He blew out another long breath. "I felt like you never cared how hard I was working to make life good for us. You never praised me or said you were proud of me. All you did was nag and put me down for not meeting your impossible expectations."

Amy felt fury rising in her chest. "*I* nagged *you* and—"

"Wait!" He held up his hands again. "I see things differently now. Please let me finish."

She knew her eyes were blazing fire, but she bit her tongue.

He stepped closer to her and put his hand on her shoulder. "Please, Amy. Let me tell you what happened next. I see everything differently now."

"Fine." She kept her arms crossed and waited.

Chris stepped back to his chair and sat. "Well, things began to change when Jim and I did this study. The Scriptures and questions forced me to face what I had been missing. I finally began to go deeper with God personally and give him control of my life, instead of trying to do it all myself. I began to see myself as God created me, and I realized I didn't have to perform to prove myself with God. He accepts me and loves me just as I am. It really hit home when I was lying in the hospital, not knowing if I would live or die. I saw how helpless I was and that my accomplishments meant nothing when it came down to what mattered—being close to God and ... and you."

Amy opened her mouth to speak, but he put up a hand again.

"I'm a long way from perfect, and I still struggle to be transparent with you. But it's like ..." He reached his hand out toward her. "I want to prioritize relationships instead of work from now on."

Amy simply stared at him. If he thought she would just forget everything in the past because he had some sort of epiphany when he thought he was dying, that was *not* happening. She felt her face redden as she let out all her built-up anger.

"You know how long I've been asking you to do a study with me? I'm your *wife*. We are supposed to be one, supposed to be learning *together* about God's plan for our marriage. I've asked you to be on this journey over and over. You wanted none of it." She swept her arm across the counter. "Then here comes Jim, a relative stranger, asking you to do a study. And just like that, you do it? Honestly?"

Chris started to speak, but it was her turn to hold up a hand.

"My turn. I listened to you, now you listen to me."

He clamped his lips together and nodded.

"That's so unfair. I feel hurt, ignored, disrespected, and unloved. Don't you know what I would have given to have you do a study with me? I feel left out. I believed we were going on this Christianity journey together. I wanted us to be hand in hand every step of the way. You wouldn't budge for *me*, but you did for someone you barely knew. You were working all the time, you shut me out of your life for years, and now you want me to just forget all the pain you caused me?"

Everything she had bottled up inside for years spewed out. She wanted to hurt him as much as he hurt her. When Chris's jaw clenched and his eyes narrowed, she stood up and moved away. "I didn't want to tell you this, but I no longer have the same feelings for you. I can't fake it anymore. I still love you, but I am not 'in love.' I don't know if I can ever get that feeling back."

She lifted her chin in defiance, waiting to hear what he'd say to that.

Without a word, he stood and stomped off to the basement, slamming the door behind him.

Yep, just like always. He hasn't changed at all. She stormed up the stairs to the safety and comfort of their bedroom.

She spent the rest of the evening alternately raging and crying. She couldn't eat and didn't want to do anything or go anywhere. She paced around, fuming, but when night came and Chris never came out of the basement, she slammed the bedroom door. She lay on the bed and pounded her fists in the pillow until she felt too weary to cry anymore. Finally, she gave in to sleep.

Chris normally found peace in his *killer* man cave, but he found no solace or enjoyment in the toys today. Instead, he spent the first half hour assaulting the punching bag to get control of his emotions. Finally, sweating and drained, his anger had ebbed to a gentle roar. He paced, venting his frustration, occasionally punching a pillow from the recliner. *Just two days ago, I gathered the courage to admit to her that I had been blind to my own faults. I told her I wanted to change, and that seemed to be enough for us to make up. She didn't admit any fault on her side, but I had plenty of fault for both of us.*

Chris remembered what Jim and Linda had told them all those months ago. "It only takes one spouse to change for the entire marriage to change." *I'm the man, and I was willing to go first. If it took brain surgery for me to come around, so be it.* He figured he'd need to give Amy some grace if she didn't jump in with a mea culpa of her own, but he really wanted to move past this moment.

Then he thought of how he'd caught her eavesdropping on his conversation with Jim today. *Listening in, so she can control me even more. Then she loses it when I try to explain.*

And she says she's fallen out of love with me. What the heck does that mean? I can't believe she's fallen out of love with me—does she understand how difficult it is to love her?

Chris knew he should have stayed and hashed it out, but he wasn't sure it would have done any good. She'd never listened to him before.

He thought about what she'd said. How many times had she begged him to do a Bible study? But she'd never said it *had* to be with her. He thought he was doing exactly what she wanted. How was he supposed to know studying the Bible only counted if he did it with her?

His mind traveled all over the place as he paced around the toys he'd filled his basement with—toys that now felt dead and joyless. *Maybe we should just get a divorce. Maybe that's what she wants.* Picking up a pillow from the couch, he chucked it across the room. *Wait, what am I thinking? I promised her I would never choose divorce as a solution to problems. My marriage can't fail like my parents' marriage did. My kids can't go through life resenting their dad like I did.* Chris picked up the pillow. *What do I do now?*

He clutched the pillow to his gut and sat down heavily. Finding no answers within himself, he bowed his head in prayer. *God, help me.* Words wouldn't come to him, so he just listened to the silence. He thought of his kids, about the same age he had been when his dad walked out. Wouldn't they feel the same gut-wrenching pain he had felt? God was nudging him to keep trying to make his marriage work. Jim and Linda came to his mind, their caring faces urging him to remember how important it was to listen to his wife without judging or defending. Chris had gone on the defensive, he hadn't acknowledged how much he'd hurt Amy, and he felt a nudge to do that now.

Glancing at the clock, he realized how late it was. He felt he should say something to Amy before she fell asleep.

He had calmed down some and thought he was ready to listen to her. He was ready to man up. Gathering up his courage and ignoring the churning in his stomach, he went upstairs. All the lights were off, and the house was quiet. She had gone to bed and was already fast asleep.

With things still unresolved, he didn't want to join her. She would be peacefully sleeping while *he* would be tossing and turning. And he reasoned, he didn't want to chance waking her, as they had an early morning appointment. He slipped off to the spare bedroom, hoping for a renewed chat come morning.

March 31

When Amy's alarm awoke her at five thirty, she discovered Chris had not come to bed. At first, she thought he had just risen early, but his side of the bed had obviously not been slept in. Fear and concern crept quickly in once more as it had a few days ago. *Had he collapsed in the basement? What if he had lain there unconscious all night?* Amy threw off the covers and bolted from the bed. As she hurried through the hall, she chastised herself for being so angry the night before. She screeched to a halt as she passed the spare bedroom. There he was—sound asleep. Amy's fury returned in an instant. *He just didn't want to sleep with me.*

She slipped past the room to her own to get ready for the day. *I can play this game too. He walked away from me, now it's up to him to make up. I'm not going first.*

She got dressed for his six-thirty CT scan. She would be forced to chauffer him to the hospital since he was prohibited from driving, but she didn't have to make small talk.

A fog had settled over Chris in the night, and he woke slowly. When he stood from the bed, he felt dizzy and had to sit again. When he felt stable enough to walk, he went down to the kitchen and found Amy sorting yesterday's mail. She avoided eye contact and said nothing.

He felt like he should say something, and a thought kept niggling at his brain. "Aren't we supposed to go to ... that place?" He felt disoriented and fought a moment of fear. But Dr. Matthews had said he might have ups and downs in his recovery. Perhaps this was just one of those moments.

Amy looked at him with a puzzled look on her face. "What do you mean?"

"You know, I have to go to ... I mean I need to get ... it's something about my brain." His voice trailed off. He knew what he wanted to say, but the words just wouldn't come. He hoped she would remember.

"Do you mean today? You have an appointment to have a repeat CT scan. We'll leave shortly." Her tone was brusque and their argument from the previous night came back to him in fits and spurts. "I think I have enough time to finish looking through the mail." She paused and looked up at him, head cocked to the side. "Are you okay?"

"Yes, I'm fine." *I'm not.*

He needed a shower and some fresh clothes, he decided. He moved back to their bedroom. After showering, he did not feel more clarity, but he joined Amy at the front door at six fifteen.

He thought about the test he was about to have as Amy backed the car from the driveway and started down the street. *What was the name of it again? I hope the results will be good.*

His thoughts were interrupted as Amy brushed the curb with the rear wheel as they turned into the parking lot. He knew they were driving his hot red car although he couldn't remember the name he had given it.

"Hey, take it easy—I don't want you to damage those rims. Curb rash can be expensive to fix, and it would be even worse if you bent the wheel." *That's weird! Thinking of potential damage to my precious car jarred words like "curb rash" to my lips, yet, for the life of me, I can't repeat the name of the test I am about to have.*

Through gritted teeth, Amy snapped back. "Maybe you should have asked your good friend Jim to drive you to this appointment. His driving is probably more to your liking."

Chris felt his stomach clench. It hadn't taken much for them to reach the boiling point again. But he needed to concentrate on this test now. *What was it called? Why can't I remember?* He got out of the car and waited for Amy to join him, but then realized she wasn't coming in. He still couldn't remember the name of the test he was supposed to have. Feeling frustrated and helpless, he walked in the door. Hopefully someone there would help him.

Amy seethed as she waited in the car for Chris. She turned the stereo on full blast, hoping to drown out her angry thoughts. When that didn't work, she tried talking out loud to no one.

"He hasn't changed at all. I bought into that sickly-sweet stuff he dished out a couple of days ago, but that was probably emotionalism after his close call in the hospital. What in the world am I supposed to do now? I've tried everything I know. Arrrgh!"

She pounded the steering wheel and screamed. The ringing of her phone caused her to squelch her anger.

"Yo," she answered, "I'm sitting here fuming about Chris and wondering what I'm supposed to do. And just like that you call. Must be fate."

"Oh no. What's wrong? Is he okay?"

Amy blew out a breath. "He's fine. Seems to be healing well enough. He's getting a repeat CT scan. The problem is us. We're back to the old patterns of bickering. It sure didn't take long. I thought he had finally changed after he came home from the hospital. He was sweet and apologetic for having walled me off. I felt like we had a new beginning. Apparently, it wasn't real or lasting. Yesterday we had a doozy of a fight and ended up sleeping in separate rooms."

Yo listened until her ranting ran its course. "Oh girl, I'm sorry to hear that. I was pulling for you two. You would think that a major challenge like you have been through would improve things. But for lots of couples, a big challenge can lead to divorce. That's what happened for me and Marcus. It was the difficulty that revealed to me just how incompatible we were. I am so much better off single."

"But ... I don't know. I can't even think of divorce right now. I don't even know what the CT scan is going to show or if his brain is even healing right." Despite having just ranted about the situation, Amy felt put off by the finality of Yo's advice. "Thanks, girlfriend. I'll talk with you later. I'm too upset over everything right now."

"Understood. You know I'm always here for you."

Amy tossed her phone back in her purse then sat tapping her chin for a few moments. She remembered passing some new apartments on the way to the hospital and wondered if she should start looking for a different place to live once Chris recovered. She didn't want to leave—it scared her to even think about the "D" word. And didn't she promise she would never go there? For a moment, fear caught in her throat, and she felt panicky. No matter how bad their marriage had been in the past, she had never thought about leaving Chris. But this intense stress was getting to her. *Was Yo right? Would ending this be better for us in the long run? Or maybe if I move out, then he would change for real. He would see how much he needs me.*

She reached into her purse and retrieved her phone again. Searching online for the apartment complex, she saw some photos of the grounds and the special prices they were advertising for the first wave of completed units. She forgot about everything else as she explored the different apartment sizes and options they offered.

Due to the pandemic, all the entrances to the medical building had been closed except for the one farthest from the car. Normally, the walk would not be any big deal, but Chris felt exhausted due to his fitful night, and his dizziness was getting worse. To top it off, his mask made it hard to breathe. He walked slowly and kept his focus on his destination until he reached it.

Tables were set up just inside the entrance, manned with masked and gloved employees ready to meet each person with questions and a thermometer. He frowned as he couldn't help but overhear an intense debate between a patient and an employee over some sort of paperwork. *Brain surgery patients do not do well with chaos.*

After checking in, he completed the long walk to the imaging department and felt a little better when he saw the daughter of one of their good friends at that registration desk. She found his appointment and checked him in for the CT scan.

Oh, yes. I remember now. A CT scan. At least it isn't an MRI in the claustrophobia-inducing steel coffin ... I mean tube.

The radiology tech completed the test in no time at all. When he finished, he asked Chris to come see him after he changed back into his street clothes.

"Mr. McGrath, I understand you had surgery to remove a subdural hematoma last week, right?"

"Yes."

"I believe your surgeon was expecting to see that your brain has expanded back into the cavity where the hematoma was. Unfortunately, that isn't what we see on the scan. Your brain has not expanded fully. I compared this scan to the first scan from last week. Unfortunately, you now have even more fluid filling the space."

He was stunned. Could he be hearing correctly?

"I'm afraid you'll have to go to the ER immediately."

Chris's head and heart started pounding at the same time. *Not again.*

He walked woodenly out of the lab, back down the long hall, and pushed past the doors, violating the six-foot social distance between himself and an elderly man. He turned into the parking lot and found his car, reaching for the passenger door.

The sound of Chris opening the car door startled Amy. She had been lost in reverie about leaving him, looking through the photos of the apartment complex, imagining herself living there alone. She jumped and quickly tossed her phone back into her purse then turned to look at him.

He didn't make eye contact but stared straight ahead.

With a quavering voice, he said, "Take me back to the ER. Apparently, I have more fluid than before the surgery."

Amy quickly started the car and began the short drive across the street to the ER without saying a word.

He spoke to the silence. "I'm worried about going back into the hospital. This seems worse than the first time when I just wanted the headaches to end. This time, I'm having trouble with words, and I'm dizzy. And I know more about how real the pandemic risk is."

"I don't want you to go back either, but we have to figure this out." She had noticed his cognitive ability had been slipping a bit this morning, but she thought it was just part of the process. She now regretted the few frozen words they'd exchanged this morning. Even though just moments ago, she'd been considering leaving him, she felt dread crept up her spine and wrap its horrifying fingers around her heart.

When she drove over a curb and almost sideswiped a car coming toward her, he stayed silent. *He must be really worried.* She didn't know what to think—so many questions were rattling around in her mind.

Pulling up in front of the ER doors felt like an uncomfortable dose of déjà vu. At least the security guard who almost had her arrested ten days ago was nowhere in sight this time. Or had it been eleven days? This time she obediently stayed in the car, reaching out and touching Chris's sleeve before he opened the door. "I'll be right here. Call me. I love you."

"I love you too." His reply sounded hollow and mechanical. And then, he was gone.

Knowing the drill, she parked in the ER lot. This time, she called Linda first. This was a time for prayer. Even a few platitudes might be welcome.

When Linda picked up, Amy didn't wait for her to finish a greeting. "You won't believe where I am." Tears flowed, and she talked right through them. "Chris had a repeat CT scan just now, and they found even more fluid.

He's back in the ER, and I'm in the ER parking lot." She didn't even try to stifle her sobs.

"Oh, dear Jesus," Linda's soft voice pleaded.

Amy blew her nose with a wrinkled-up tissue she found in a corner of her purse. "And that's not the worst of it. You remember a few days ago when I told you about our sweet moment together? Well, we went from heaven on earth to pure hell in just a few hours. I thought we were finally on the same page and things would be perfect going forward. I couldn't stop singing all morning. But I overheard Chris talking to Jim about a study they had done together. I overreacted. I felt so left out and alone."

She gave way to all her pent-up emotions. "Why wouldn't he do a study with me? Why wouldn't he share his spiritual life with me? Instead, he did this with Jim. I like Jim and all, don't get me wrong. But I felt left out. Anyway, we had a big fight. I was furious with Chris, and I said some horrible things. He responded just like the old Chris, putting up a wall and walking away."

She cleared her throat, unable to stop the torrent of words. "He spent the rest of the evening in the basement doing God knows what. I went to bed early. When I woke up, I discovered he'd slept in the spare room. Now I feel awful. How could I have treated him like that? He's back in the hospital, and I don't know if he will ever come out. I don't know if I will ever *see* him again." She broke down and couldn't continue.

Linda's soothing voice came over the phone. "I'm here for you, and I'm sorry this is happening. There is much we don't understand. But none of this is a mystery to God. Chris loves you, and he knows you love him. Your argument is going to be a tiny blip on the horizon years from now. Can I pray for you?"

Amy whispered yes, and Linda began. "Oh Lord, Chris and Amy are in a deep, dark valley right now. They don't know which end is up. But you do. Fear cannot conquer them if you are by their side, and we know you are. Please lead Chris and Amy through the mess, the brain problem, the conflict, and their pain. Please fill them each with your strength and peace. May your comfort take away their fear and loneliness. Amen."

Amy felt the tiniest bit of warmth and stillness begin to grow inside her. Her head stopped pounding, and she took a deep breath. "What am I going to do now?"

"God will show you, but it's often just one step at a time. We're here for you, whatever you need. Can we tentatively plan for me to come for a visit tomorrow? We can sit six feet apart and process all this. By then, you will have heard from the doctor and have an idea of what is going on. Remember, the doctor is excellent and has such a good reputation. Let him do his job. Rest, eat, and stay clearheaded. Chris needs you to be strong for him. God will give you strength if you ask."

They hung up, and a few seconds later, her phone buzzed with another call. She saw the call was from the hospital exchange and eagerly answered, heart pounding.

"Hello, Mrs. McGrath. It's Dr. Matthews. I wanted to call you right away and tell you there's no need to wait in the parking lot. We are admitting your husband for a few days so we can monitor the new fluid. We are going to send him for another MRI with contrast tonight. That should provide a better picture of what we are dealing with.

"There will be other tests as well. Sometimes we see this after surgery, so you shouldn't be too worried at this point. It's a watch and wait process. People's brains produce fluid after surgery, which is why we inserted the drain. You will recall he seemed to generate less fluid than normal after surgery. More fluid developed after the drain was removed, and he was discharged. The fluid sometimes dissipates naturally. At this point, I don't have any reason to think I will need to do another surgery."

His calm, reassuring words did wonders for Amy's pounding heart.

"That helps a lot. Thank you for calling me so quickly. I didn't know what to do." Her brain could not comprehend another surgery, but the doctor sounded so confident, she felt reassured.

"You're welcome. Please go back home now and don't worry. Prayers are good too. I will call after we have more to report."

With nothing left to do, Amy shifted the car into reverse and slowly backed out, leaving the other people sitting in their cars by themselves. She thought of the other patients forced to face everything alone. Expressions of love and familiarity had been quarantined too.

All day, her thoughts accused her. She tried to eat, but only forced a little soup down. When darkness fell, she took a cup of tea to her room and changed into her pajamas. But the warmth of her empty bed chilled her heart. Thoughts swirled around in an endless vortex, condemning her.

How stupid could I be? How could I have been that selfish and mean? He was barely recovering when he reached out to me, and I threw a hissy fit. Maybe I caused him to regress. What if it's my fault he's in the ER? What if he doesn't recover? I know better than to give up on my marriage. What was I thinking?

April 1

Amy rolled over for the umpteenth time and noticed it was two o'clock in the morning. It was the first day of April. *Am I the April fool?*

She rehashed the past few days, remembering Chris's tears and tender words when she woke to find him downstairs. He'd asked for her forgiveness! She recalled his animated voice as he talked to Jim about the study and how much he had learned. She could still see his shocked face when she confronted him with her jealousy. His earnest pleading for her to understand came back to her now. And she remembered how his loving face became like ice-cold flint when she spewed out her immature responses.

She went downstairs to find the Bible study Chris had been doing. Sitting on the sofa in the same place she had found him a few days ago, she paged through the book. There were many notes he had written in the margins.

"I know I measure up at work, everyone respects me, but what's their motivation? I've never measured up with the people who mean the most to me. My dad or Amy. It's hard to look them in the eye. God, I know you can change all that. At least you believe in me. Give me courage to walk away from this shame."

She continued going through the book, stopping to read a note here, an underlined phrase there. The words seemed to be written by someone else, not the man she thought she knew. This man was thoughtful and deep. Repentant. Vulnerable and hurt. She remembered the Chris she knew in the early days, the one who risked his life to jump out of the raft to save her. He was willing to do *anything* for her. He was still that same man deep down inside, only something had caused him to hide his feelings.

For the first time, she realized how she had triggered shame in him, and of course that would compel him to clam up in their angry moments. He couldn't trust her with his innermost thoughts. She wasn't a safe person for him. Sorrow gripped her heart when she realized she had hurt him. Chris would do anything for her. What could she do for him?

The key was in me all along.

The thought startled her. Of course, she had been blind to her own faults. *The key was in me all along. I'm only responsible for my actions. God, I've been so foolish. I blamed Chris for my own faults. Will you forgive me? Will you show me how to untangle this mess I've made? I love you, and I love my husband.*

She sat with the book in her lap, lost in thought. She felt God's approval, and that lifted the sorrow from her heart. Her breath came slower and deeper, and she finally felt sleepy. She pulled her legs up, snuggled under the throw, and clutched the book to her chest. As her heavy head dropped to the arm of the sofa, her thoughts slowed to a trickle, and her eyelids closed in sleep.

Amy's eyes opened as the first pink of morning was brightening up the family room. It took her a few moments to realize where she was. She could see the picture window framing what promised to be a beautiful sunrise. Unfurling her legs, she sat up and noticed the Bible study book was still in her hands. The thoughts of last night seemed fresh in her mind. *The key was in me all along.*

After breakfast, Linda came to visit as promised. They sat six feet apart on the lanai, bundled in warm coats to protect them from the winter that never seemed to end. Steaming cups of tea kept their hands warm. A fire crackled in the fireplace, but its heat barely warmed them as Amy recounted what had happened between her and Chris. This time she had no interest in focusing on his faults but was compelled to be honest and transparent with Linda for the first time.

"I know why we were at such an impasse. Chris was operating from a position of deep shame, and I was adding layers to his shame. Why did I think he could trust me enough to be vulnerable when my words proved I couldn't be? I criticized him constantly. When he retreated, I criticized him more." Amy looked down into her tea, swirling the cup a little and watching the ripples in the surface. Then she looked back up at Linda. "I believed our problems were all his fault. I only focused on *my* needs. I never considered what *his* needs might be. I know our problems are multilayered and complex, and he has issues he needs to address. But those aren't my responsibility. From my standpoint, the key to healing our relationship was in *me* all along."

Linda smiled warmly. "What a major discovery. It's insightful of you. Thank you for trusting me enough to share it with me."

"But now what do I do? Will I ever be able to win his trust back? How in the world do I change? It's impossible to take back all the horrible things I said." Amy's voice faltered. "And I may never be able to. He's in the hospital again, and I don't know if he's ever coming back."

"Don't ever believe there's no chance to fix things. Up to your last breath on earth, there is a way. You will find it if you seek it. I have a feeling there will be plenty of time. The Bible is full of stories of people who changed dramatically. They almost became another person with a totally new identity. And most often, all it took was one little decision to start the ball rolling. Like the story of Sarah."

"Hmm, Sarah. You mean Sarah and Abraham? I don't know much about her." She took a sip of her tea.

Linda nodded. "Sarah eventually became known to have a 'gentle and quiet spirit.' But it hadn't always been her nature. Her name at birth was Sarai, meaning 'princess.' She was wealthy and privileged, and she was anything but gentle and quiet. She was married to Abram, a man with a great destiny marked out for him by God. He was to be the father of many nations. But for decades, Sarai was barren. The couple had unhealthy patterns in their lives. Abram wasn't sure of himself and didn't believe he was marked out for greatness. Because of this, several times he came close to losing everything God had destined for him. Sarai didn't see his greatness either, she saw someone she could control to get the things she wanted. She shamed her husband into doing some crazy things to have an heir, and when it didn't work out, she blamed him for the outcome. They had a totally dysfunctional household. They could have lost their opportunity to be all they were intended to be." Linda took a last sip from her cup and set it down on the table.

"What happened then? Did Sarai find the key was in her?"

"That's one way to say it. We don't know all the personal details of what went on between Sarai and Abram, but we do know things started to change. After decades of waiting to become parents ... they were well past childbearing age ... a new promise was made to them. Abram and Sarai received new names to match their new identities from God. The new identities were what they were destined to be all along, only they weren't living as if they knew it. Sarai's new name was Sarah, which means 'mother of nations.'"

Amy frowned. "What an odd identity for a barren woman."

"Yes, except the prophecy did come true. They became parents and established the whole nation of Israel. I think Sarah's turning point came when she saw herself as she was designed to be. When our giftedness is named, and we give place to who we are created to be, we can be inspired to live up to our destiny. And a deep affection and devotion to our Creator is birthed in us for giving us that unique identity."

As Linda rose to put another log on the fire, Amy thought about everything she'd said. Thinking of others fulfilling their God-given destiny delighted her, but she struggled to think of how she could find her own. Amy admitted, "I don't know who I am, Linda. What is my identity?"

"We all struggle with that question." Linda sat once more and nodded. "The Bible says God formed each one of us in our mother's womb. He designed us uniquely with a specific identity and purpose. So, he alone knows the answer to your question."

Amy felt her heart quicken at this news. She'd always thought she was the one who decided her own destiny, but ... she didn't choose to be born. And she didn't design herself. If God formed her with an identity and purpose, it would make sense that he would be the only one who knew what it was. Was it possible she had a God-designed purpose? Would he reveal it to her?

"How do I find out from God what it is?" Amy leaned forward, eager to hear Linda's answer.

"You ask him."

"But ... but does he speak? Out loud? Or ... I don't know how I would hear his answer."

Linda's eyes sparkled. "When you made the decision to serve Jesus with your whole heart, the spirit of God came to live inside of you. He has been speaking to you all along, but perhaps you didn't realize it was him. You probably attributed his words to your own thoughts or your conscience. That was true for me before I began to patiently listen to him." She reached for the teapot and refilled her cup. "I would be driving by a homeless person and have this strong urge to stop and give them some money. Or I would interrupt Jim when he was talking and later feel compelled to apologize. It is one way the Spirit speaks ... nudging us to do something. But he also answers our prayers directly."

Amy bit her lip. She had experienced nudges to do things—and most often ignored them. *Was that God trying to talk to me?*

Linda leaned forward in her seat. "When you ask God for wisdom, just speak in your own words, asking that his voice is the only voice you will hear. Always remember to journal what you are seeing, hearing, and feeling. His timing isn't the same as ours, and it may not be the right time for you to know everything. You can look back in your journal and see the meaning of a message clearly after a time."

"I'm looking forward to listening to God. There are so many questions I have for him. I desperately want to know how to make things right between Chris and me. And I know I must start with me. I'm not sure what to do, but I believe God will show me."

"Yes, he will. Hold on a sec." Linda dug around in her purse and pulled out a small booklet. "Here's some information for you. It will help you learn how to hear God's voice. Remember, Jim and I will continue praying for you both. Especially for this new development with the fluid on Chris's brain. In fact, let me pray for you right now before I go."

Linda's prayer flowed over Amy in peaceful waves despite the distance they kept. After Linda said "amen" and left, Amy picked up the booklet and put it on the coffee table to read later.

All day, Amy kept busy calling and emailing to keep everyone updated. Friends and family were astounded to hear Chris was back in the hospital and expressed their support and devotion to prayer. When she'd finished, she tried to watch some TV to decompress, but decided she couldn't watch the news anymore. Seeing the same video clips of hospital personnel and gurneys being wheeled into emergency rooms with pandemic-infected patients increased her stress level.

She talked to Chris on the phone a couple of times and texted throughout the day. He had a headache again, but it wasn't too bad. He did seem a little foggy, though, and his words came out slowly. She thought he seemed tired, so their conversations were brief.

She also had another call with Dr. Matthews, who let her know there hadn't been much change from the night before.

"The fluid we saw in the CT scan is not blood, which means there is no active bleeding. That's good. Remember, a chronic subdural hematoma is a collection of blood and fluid encapsulated by what we call a membrane. In the surgery, I was able to remove most of this membrane. We had to leave some of it behind because it was too close to delicate areas of the brain where we couldn't be as aggressive. The remaining membranes would normally be absorbed by the body over time. For some reason, there is a copious amount of fluid in his skull. We think this could be due to something we refer to as 'leaky membranes.'"

She tapped her pen on her chin. "So far I am following, but what do you recommend now?"

"We have three options. We could insert another drain, or we could wait and see if the fluid dissipates on its own. Finally, we could do another craniotomy to remove the fluid. I prefer to hold off on deciding. Give us twenty-four hours. I have three other neurosurgeons consulting with me on his case, and we'll keep a close watch on your husband and continue to monitor the fluid levels. I'm going to give you my cell phone number in case you need to reach me."

She wrote rapidly as he spoke. *A neurosurgeon is giving me his personal phone number? He is so caring. Or ... or is Chris that desperately ill?* She felt sick. If Dr. Matthews had to consult three other neurosurgeons, something was very wrong.

Later that evening, she felt a nudge to study the booklet Linda gave her. She sat on the sofa and read through it quickly. The information reinforced what Linda had already told her about ways to hear God communicating with her. She decided to try it out—ask God a question and see what response she got. She prepared by sitting comfortably, taking several deep breaths, and relaxing. She prayed the prayer from the booklet out loud.

"Father, in the name of Jesus and according to Matthew 28:18 and Luke 10:19–20, I take authority over this room and ask that your Spirit would remove any influence over me that is not from you. According to 2 Corinthians 10:5, I place my own thoughts and imagination under your control in obedience to you. Thank you, God, for this truth and your power. Amen."

Then she took a deep breath and started the conversation. *What do you want me to know about my marriage?*

She closed her eyes and waited. After a few moments, she imagined a gorgeous white horse coming toward her with its reins dangling down. As the horse came nearer, she grabbed hold of the reins. Then the horse disappeared but she was still holding the reins. She didn't understand what this meant. *What do you want me to know about this, God?*

In her mind, she envisioned another scene. She stood beside a river that was shaded by a forest of trees. Streaks of sunlight danced through the leaves and bounced off the water. Then she saw Jesus walking out of the trees, holding out his hands to her. His face was welcoming, glad to see her. She ran to him, and he put his arm around her. He pointed across the river to two paths coming up out of the water and up a mountain.

She saw Chris on one path and herself on the other. At the top of the mountain, she saw the two paths converging together with a sparkling white cross standing at that spot. She saw that as she and Chris followed their separate paths, they both grew closer to Jesus and closer to each other. Their destinies came together when they reached him.

She knew at that moment what the other visual meant. She had been trying to force Chris to take her path, her way. The more she tried to force him, the farther apart they grew. But he was designed for his path, not hers. And she had to take her path alone. She understood the reins symbolized her attitude toward Chris, trying to control him. In the vision, she looked down and saw the reins still in her hands. She knew what to do. She handed the reins to Jesus. As soon as they touched his hands, they vanished.

She looked up at her Lord and Savior and asked about her identity and purpose. His smile flooded her with warmth, and she felt the words more than heard them. *You are my beloved daughter. You are my treasure. I chose you to be filled with my love and to let it flow out to those around you.*

She never wanted to leave his side.

She felt complete in his presence and savored the joy bubbling up in her. After a while, the scene slowly faded, but her heart overflowed with emotion. As she refocused on where she was in her living room, she knew what she had to do. When she was ready, she retrieved a new journal and wrote down what she had experienced.

Linda was right. Hearing God's words increased her devotion to him and inspired her to live up to her identity. Now that she felt his healing love filling her, she wanted to share that love with everyone else. But first she would work on getting rid of the things that prevented her from feeling his love—her selfishness, anger, and control issues. She didn't ever want to pick up those reins again.

That night, she lay in bed not knowing if Chris was going to live or die, and yet she felt perfect peace filling her heart. She couldn't understand it, but she knew that kind of peace came from above. *Thank you. Thank you so much, Lord!* When she closed her eyes, she could still see Jesus smiling at her.

April 2

Early the next morning, Amy received a call from Chris. She longed to tell him what she learned from Jesus, but after they talked for a little while, she decided this wasn't the best time. She noticed he occasionally stumbled over his words. This development concerned her, but she didn't mention it to him. He put the call on speakerphone when Dr. Matthews entered the room.

Dr. Matthews patiently reviewed yesterday's first option. "We discussed inserting a new drain, but when I examined Chris, I realized that will not be possible without surgery. His scalp is very thick."

She giggled. "I always knew you had a thick head."

Dr. Matthews interjected. "Chris, I've heard that from my wife too."

Both men laughed.

"The second option was to wait for the fluid to dissipate. We could send him to rehab either here in the hospital or at home. While he is getting speech and physical therapy, the fluid could have time to dissipate. The risk with that option is surgery may still be required later if the fluid doesn't dissipate as quickly as we would like. And we would be working against time since the pandemic surge doesn't seem to be slowing down. In a meeting this morning, hospital administration estimated we could be 100 percent full of pandemic patients just eight days from now."

Amy felt stunned at this news and spoke up when Chris didn't. "One hundred percent full of pandemic patients? What will happen to him if this dire prediction comes true?"

"I don't have a good answer for you at this point. We are working on a day-to-day basis. Many people are busy behind the scenes developing plans and trying to adjust to an unstable situation."

She continued. "That option sounds both hopeful and terrifying. What other options are there?"

"The third option is to do a repeat surgery right away to remove the fluid. The longer the fluid remains in the subdural cavity, the more pressure and possible damage there is to the brain. However, this option has a risk as well. A repeat surgery this close in time has a much higher chance of infection. The other neurosurgeons I've consulted with all believe we should avoid a second surgery if possible."

Amy had heard enough to make her decision. "I think we should go with option two then. Rehab would be good for him now and might get him home faster. Meanwhile, you can monitor him and make sure the fluid isn't increasing, right?"

"Absolutely. If he's in the hospital rehab, I can visit him each day. We'll make sure he continues to have CT scans to monitor the fluid level."

"That sounds like a good choice then. Chris, what do you think? Would you prefer to go to rehab and skip another surgery?"

"Yeah."

Her husband didn't elaborate, and she wondered if he was tracking the conversation. "Great. Dr. Matthews, is there anything we need to do to help get him moved to rehab?"

"No, we can handle everything here. They'll make sure there's room for him, and your insurance will cover it."

Amy felt optimistic about the decision. Sure, there were risks. But hadn't they already been through so much? It just had to work out for the best.

After lunch, she decided to get out and take a walk, heading down to the park. There was a hint of spring in the air and just stepping outside of the house lifted her spirits. Maybe this miserable winter was going to end after all.

She saw several neighbors on her way to the park who all knew about Chris. Word traveled fast in this small town. Everyone was concerned about him, and that comforted her. She couldn't hug anyone, of course, and their faces were masked. But just being in the presence of other people lifted her spirits greatly. It was nice to be away from her empty house.

The park was starting to show signs of spring—yellow buds were popping out on the forsythia bushes, the ice on the creek was only clinging here and there to its banks. She took the bridge over the creek and walked to "their" bench—the one where Chris had proposed. Trudging over the still-brown grass, she sat down. The scene looked so beautiful with the sunlight dancing on the ripples of the creek as it slipped past the boulders. The soothing sounds and her memories of this place gave her peace. She sensed everything was under control even though she couldn't see it. She found breathing room. Her racing thoughts slowed to a trickle.

Her peace lasted only a few short minutes before her phone rang. Linda was calling to let her know Jim had just talked to Chris.

"Jim thought Chris sounded really off—he couldn't really hold a conversation. Before they hung up, Chris said, 'Bye, Bob.'"

"What? That's disturbing." Amy paused before saying, "When I last spoke to him, I also noticed he stumbled with a few words. I'll call him, and if he seems to be worse than earlier this morning, I'll call his surgeon." She blew out a breath. "Thanks for letting me know—being separated from him makes it challenging to know what's really going on. I appreciate all the input I can get."

Amy rose from the bench and paced as she listened to the phone ringing. Finally, she heard Chris's voice on the other end.

"Hi, babe." She tried to keep her voice positive and upbeat, deliberately speaking slowly and clearly. "How do you feel?"

"Not good. Um … tired." The words seemed more garbled than just hours ago.

"Did you have lunch yet?"

"Yeah."

"What did you have?"

There was a long pause, then he mumbled, "I dunno."

"Do you want to sleep now?"

"Yeah."

"Okay, I'll let you go then. I'll talk to you later. I love you." She forced herself to sound upbeat for his sake but found herself feeling as if a weight were pressing down on her.

"Yeah." She could hear some rustling and fumbling until the call was cut off.

He is not okay.

She bit her lip as she looked through her contacts and found Dr. Matthews's cell number. She left a breathless message, then hurried toward home. Sitting now felt impossible. Moving calmed her nervous energy.

In a few minutes, Dr. Matthews called. She stepped off the path by a tree and answered.

"I was just about to call you when I saw you had left a message. I stopped by to see Chris a few minutes ago and noticed he is much less cognizant than earlier. He's sleepy as well, and his reflexes aren't as good on the right side. These are signs that the irritation to his brain is increasing. I asked if he agreed we should do surgery. He agreed. I have him scheduled for eight-thirty tomorrow morning. I'll check in with the surgeons I'm consulting, but I'm sure they will concur. Do you have any objections?"

"No. I think he needs surgery too. I've been alarmed at the change in him since this morning, and a friend who spoke to him said the same thing. Are you sure you can wait until morning?"

"We'll do another CT to give us the latest information. They'll most likely do the scan this evening. But he's being closely monitored in the ICU, and if anything changes, they'll call me. I fully expect it will be okay to wait, but I'm also convinced that doing a repeat craniotomy is necessary. Unfortunately, you won't be able to come to the hospital for this surgery. No family members are allowed in at this point. I'll FaceTime with you in the morning before the surgery so you can see him. And I'll call you when the surgery is done to let you know how it went."

Amy felt fear growing in the pit of her stomach. "It's going to be horrible not to be there. But we trust you, Dr. Matthews. Thank you."

She slumped back heavily against the tree and closed her eyes. She was scared, and her hands were trembling. Just a few minutes ago, as she studied the creek, she felt everything was under control. But now she felt helpless and powerless. She paused as a thought occurred to her. *Curious, that figure of speech "under control." Whose control am I under?* Her emotions were on a roller coaster. One moment she had her act together, and the next, she was falling apart. She imagined God above having everything "under control" because his vision was much broader and wider than hers. He was never helpless or powerless. She could trust him.

Thank you, God, for the word picture. I choose to trust you with Chris's situation.

She stood in silence, feeling peace fill her heart, knowing only God could help Chris—and he would. She saw another bench nearby and sat, soaking in the sunshine and watching two squirrels chasing each other up and down the trees. She needed some extra reserves in her emotional tank for the long night ahead of her. As she crossed her legs, she noticed she was also getting thinner. *When did I eat last?*

After resting for a few minutes, she got up and went home. There was a long list of people to text, call, and email to update and to ask for prayer. She forced herself to eat a power bar and drink a tall glass of ice water. Then she curled up on the sofa and prepared to make her calls. She decided to start with Linda.

Linda picked up immediately. "Hi. Did you have a chance to talk to Chris? How does he sound to you?"

This time the sound of Linda's voice didn't make her weep. She felt calm. "He is not doing well at all. He's stumbling over his words, and it's much worse than it was this morning. His right side is also weaker than the left. They're going to do another surgery tomorrow morning."

"Oh my! Oh no ... I'm so sorry. We didn't expect this at all." Her mentor sighed and paused for a moment. "Even though this setback has thrown you for a loop, I can assure you that God is with him. And with you."

Amy closed her eyes and remembered Jesus's arm of comfort around her shoulder.

After her phone call with Linda, Amy contacted their kids and close family but resorted to sending an email to the rest of the people she needed to update. She didn't have the time, but she also didn't have the energy. Linda and Jim promised to give the prayer team the details. After one more call to Chris's nurse for an update, she knew he was stable and being watched over. Now she needed some TLC.

She made a big cup of herbal tea and carried it up to their bedroom. She looked through Chris's closet and found the old T-shirt he wore to bed. She held the tee up to her nose and inhaled his scent. Putting it on, she instantly felt comforted. She turned on her diffuser, which filled the air with her favorite blend of essential oils. She got into bed and found a video to play on her TV of a crackling fire in a beautiful fireplace. The video was eight hours long. *That should be enough.* Last, but not least, she picked up her Bible, dusty from lack of use, and her journal.

Okay, God, I'm here, I'm listening, and I'm ready. I desperately need to feel peace. My mind is a jumble of worried thoughts. I'm exhausted. I'm afraid. I'm not doing well with this.

She sat in silence, stilling her body and mind, focusing on God. Soon, she felt a sense of inner peace radiating through her body. She imagined Jesus sitting in a raft in front of her, his strong arms controlling the vessel through a rough river. She remembered her terror when they'd taken the whitewater rafting trip all those years ago, and Hunter had been their guide. This was totally different. The atmosphere in the raft was quiet and still even though the surrounding scene was chaos. Then they were on land. Jesus sat on the ground on top of a rounded hill, smiling at her, inviting her to join him. The birds were singing, and the sky was blue. She sat down facing her Savior and soaked up the love in his eyes. The compassion and strength she saw in his gaze entranced her.

She didn't know how long she sat in meditation, but with each breath she felt more alive and more at peace. The endless striving for control slipped off her tense shoulders, and her muscles relaxed to their natural positions. She willingly submitted to being under God's control. Her breathing slowed and deepened, sending life-giving oxygen throughout her body.

She turned to her Bible and opened her journal. She read Psalm 23, and when she sensed his words of encouragement, she wrote them down. They gave her such hope. Reuniting with her long-lost friend was going to take some time. Apparently, longer than her eyes would be able to remain open tonight as she began nodding off at intervals.

Putting away her Bible and journal, she slipped under the covers and sank into a deep sleep.

April 3. Morning

As Amy felt herself awaken, she savored the feeling of rejuvenation and rest. Her shoulders felt relaxed, their ever-present knots only small tangles now. She rolled over to look at her phone and was surprised to see it was past seven o'clock already. She must have slept right through the alarm. She sat up in bed, suddenly fully awake and aware of what day it was.

Normally, Chris would have called by now. She punched in his number, and let it ring until it went to voice mail. She frowned. After a quick trip to the bathroom, she jumped back under the covers and tried again. No answer. Had he been taken to the imaging department for another CT scan? Had his cell phone battery died?

She looked up the number for his bedside phone and tried that. She knew it was near shift change, but she had to find out what was going on. A woman picked up the call after two rings.

Oh good, one of the nurses. "Good morning, this is Mrs. McGrath. How is Chris this morning? I've tried calling him twice, but he didn't pick up."

"Hello, Mrs. McGrath. This is Anna, one of your husband's nurses. He is extremely sleepy this morning. He was stable all night, but he's hardly verbal now. They took him down for a CT scan earlier and didn't see any new concerns. After the surgery this morning, they will do an EEG to monitor for seizures. Dr. Matthews just arrived. One minute please." There was a long pause. "The doctor will call you back shortly."

Amy only had time to mumble, "Of course" before the line went dead. *What was happening?* She jumped out of bed and raced to pull on jeans, a sweatshirt, and warm socks.

Her cell phone rang, and she picked it up, settling onto the love seat in the bedroom.

"Good morning, it's Dr. Matthews. I stopped by to see Chris before prepping for surgery. He is having trouble staying awake, just opens his eyes temporarily when we say his name. He is not speaking at all, and his right arm isn't moving. He doesn't appear to have any feeling in it and is not able to hold it up. He is not well, neurologically speaking. It was an incredibly good decision to schedule surgery this morning. We've alerted the neurologist, and we'll be monitoring your husband for any possible seizures, which are quite common when the brain is irritated. I only have a few minutes before I get ready for surgery. Do you have any questions?"

Fear rose inside her like a tidal wave as she tried to keep up with documenting his words. "No, I don't have any questions."

"I'll put the nurse back on so she can get your permission for the surgery."

This was something new—they hadn't asked her for permission for the last surgery. She guessed Chris was not able to give permission himself. *This sounds ominous.*

Nurse Anna came back on the phone and got her verbal consent for Dr. Matthews to do the craniotomy. She numbly replied to all of Anna's questions. Then Dr. Matthews's friendly voice came back on the line.

"I'm sorry you can't be here for this surgery. Would it be okay if I prayed now?"

"Yes, please."

Dr. Matthews calmly asked the Great Physician for power, patience, and peace for their family. He said goodbye and hung up right after her *amen*.

Panic crushed Amy as she envisioned the worst. Her imagination took over, filling her mind with tragic scenarios. She put her head into her hands and wailed, feeling helpless and hopeless.

I need you now, God. Help me! How much more can I endure?

Minutes passed, and each one brought more painful laments. She had never felt as alone, terrified, or remorseful. Chris was unreachable now, unable to speak or comprehend what was happening. She might never see his face again. He was in the hands of strangers, and his life hung in the balance. Four brain surgeons were baffled by his mysterious condition.

The last time the two of them were together, they were both so angry they barely spoke. They hadn't even slept in the same bed on their last night together. The words she spat at him that day seared her heart like a hot, surging stream of toxic lava.

She curled up on the love seat in a heap, sobs racking her body. She let it all out until she couldn't cry anymore. Then she lay there, numb and broken.

Suddenly her phone rang. Startled, she picked it up and was surprised to see it was Dr. Matthews. She quickly swiped at her wet face and answered.

"Hello?"

No one answered.

"Hello?"

Still nothing. In the background, she could detect the sound of Dr. Matthews's voice along with a second voice, a woman. As she listened, she gradually realized Dr. Matthews hadn't meant to call her. He must have set his phone down in the room where he was preparing for surgery and accidentally redialed her number. She focused on the voices. She couldn't make out exactly what they were saying, but she could detect the tone.

These voices weren't appalled and lamenting and terrified like hers. These voices were calm, professional, and businesslike. She imagined they were getting supplies or equipment ready. As they moved about the room, the volume of their voices rose and fell, sounding extremely focused and confident. This gave her reassurance Chris was in good hands.

Each second made her feel more comforted and confident she could trust this good doctor to take care of her husband. She sat up straighter and her tears dried up. She grabbed a tissue to blot her face.

Many more minutes passed, and finally, Dr. Matthews's voice got much louder and clearer. "Hello? Who's there?"

"Dr. Matthews, it's Amy McGrath. You must have accidentally redialed me."

"What? That's crazy, I'm sorry."

"No, no, don't be sorry at all."

"I'll be in touch after the surgery."

As he disconnected the call, she realized something. Her cry to God, her ever-present help, had been answered immediately. She imagined, at the sound of her plea, angels had been sent flying to the hospital to initiate that phone call. The unsuspecting doctor had no idea his phone had placed that call for ten long minutes. Those minutes and the sound of his professional voice had given Amy exactly the comfort she needed.

Her heart was soothed and softened, knowing God was right there with her. And also with Chris. She sighed ... a long, deep, satisfying sigh.

April 3. Afternoon

With a bucket of warm sudsy water next to her, Amy reached up and wiped the wooden window blinds, beginning with the top slat. The rag quickly became dirty, and she bent down to rinse it out and begin again. The blinds had been crying out for a good cleaning for months, maybe years. She put her body and soul to work, attempting to keep on the go to pass the time. Cleaning kept her hands busy, and worship tunes kept her soul engaged as she sang at the top of her voice.

Maybe Linda was right about how therapeutic cleaning could be. More and more it seemed that Linda was right about many things.

A couple of hours later, Amy had sung through her entire worship library and started it again as she moved systematically through the windows in her house. Sunlight streamed in through the dining room windows now, its warmth increasing her sunny mood. The last window was almost complete when the music stopped abruptly, and her phone announced an incoming call. She eagerly put down her cleaning supplies and answered. Dr. Matthews was requesting to FaceTime with her. *Finally.*

She saw the doctor's face on the screen. "There's someone here who wants to talk to you." The image jostled as the doctor adjusted the phone to show Chris's face. Her husband looked sleepy and sported a huge new bandage in the same spot as the first one.

She felt a surge of love at seeing his face again. "Hi. How do you feel?"

"Fine. How ... are ... you?" He tried to smile. His voice was raspy and thick, but he was talking.

She laughed because he wanted to know how *she* was. She didn't know if he was joking or slightly confused, but she enjoyed the interaction either way.

"I'm doing well, thanks for asking." She spoke formally to test if it had been a joke. When he didn't laugh, she moved on. "You have an exceptionally good doctor. Do you know that?"

"Yes ... sleepy now." He struggled to keep his eyes open.

There was her answer—he was still groggy and tired. "I love you, and I'll talk to you again soon."

Dr. Matthews flipped the camera back to himself. "He is still drowsy, but I wanted to call you as soon as possible to let you see him. The surgery was successful. You heard him talking, and his right side is stronger now. Those are both positive signs."

"Why was he unable to speak or stay awake this morning? That was scary." She had retrieved her notebook to record the doctor's impressions.

"We wondered if he had been having seizures and planned on getting a neurologist involved if his speech and motor function didn't bounce back after the surgery. But they did. My assumption is his brain was excessively irritated and inflamed due to how quickly the fluid had increased. It was affecting the parts of his brain which control speech and movement on the upper right side."

Amy nodded as she recorded his findings. "I'm learning more about how the brain works. What else did you find in this surgery?"

"The membrane remnants from the last surgery had not been absorbed by the body. Instead, they had grown and seemed to be the source of the fluid which filled the open space and prevented the brain from fully expanding as it should have. But that also made them easier to remove this time."

She nodded again. "Yes, I remember you mentioned those membranes that had surrounded the hematoma."

"After the evacuation, we saw the brain bounce back quickly. It was much more dramatic than the first surgery, which is an encouraging development. But the membranes also looked unusual, so I sent a sample to the pathology department just to be safe."

"That's good to hear that his brain bounced back." She put down her pen. "Thank you, Dr. Matthews. How long do you expect him to stay?"

"We'll take it slow. I put two drains in this time which are designed to create greater suction. We want to be sure when he goes home it will be for good. I can't give you an exact date, but he'll have to stay at least four days."

"I understand. I want him to be fully well when he comes back."

"We'll put him back into the makeshift ICU. It's the only one for non-pandemic patients. But we'll find the quietest place we can. Also, the nurse can give him earplugs and eyeshades to make it easier to sleep at night. We'll do all we can to make sure he is as comfortable as possible."

She thanked Dr. Matthews profusely for his positive update, and they ended the call.

What a roller coaster we have been on. Hours ago, I was wailing, and now I feel like dancing. This morning he couldn't speak or stay awake, and now he's talking. How incredible. We are finally on the road to recovery. Thank you, God!

She closed her eyes for a brief second of praise then realized she better start making calls again. Before she could place a call or send an email, her cell rang.

She smiled as she answered. "Hi, Jon. You and Jackie have a knack for knowing when I need a friend to talk to."

"Well, your emails have helped us know when you might need some cheering up. And God's timing is perfect. We assumed the surgery would be complete by now. How did it go?"

"Yes, he's out of surgery. It's amazing how much better he is already. His neurosurgeon believes the second surgery should do the trick, but it's still early."

"That's an incredible answer to prayer. Especially considering the past few days. Your emails had us really concerned. How are you doing?"

"I'm good with his medical condition, but I'm sorry I was so quick to get off the phone when we last spoke. Things weren't so good between Chris and me before this began, and I just chose not to get into that."

"You *are* dealing with a lot. Chris and I traded a few voice mails in the last year or so, but we never actually talked. I did wonder if something was off between you two because he seemed reluctant to connect. How about if I pray for you?"

Amy felt her pent-up tension melt away. "Yes, I would appreciate that."

"Lord Jesus, you know all about the struggles our friends are dealing with, both physically and in their relationship. You are the Great Physician and can heal both. I pray for that, trusting for a miracle. Amen."

"Amen," Amy echoed. "Thanks, Jon. Please continue to pursue Chris. I'm sure he would be open to talking once he gets back home."

"I'll definitely do that."

When the call ended, Amy sat down and stared out the window. *Bringing our challenges out into the open with our friend wasn't as bad as I feared. It sure helps to have people praying for us. Jon and Jackie are such good friends.*

Chris awakened, blinking the sleep from his eyes. *Where am I?* He was propped on his side, limiting his vision, and he couldn't roll over. At first, that bothered him, but the thought soon faded away. In front of him were pale green floor-to-ceiling curtains drawn around his bed. He was mesmerized as he watched them swaying slightly every time someone walked by. He lay there for the longest time just gazing at them, blinking slowly.

After a few moments, a nurse came bustling in. She rolled the vital signs monitor cart next to his bed, then entered something on the keyboard. "Looks like you're awake, Mr. McGrath. Can you tell me your birthday?"

"March 5, 1970," came his immediate reply.

"Very good. Do you know where you are?"

He glanced around. "At the hospital. Am I in the makeshift ICU again?"

"Yes, you are. Do you know what day it is?"

He tried to think, but his head hurt. Well, he had a birthday right before all this happened, and that was in March. He ventured a guess. "April something?"

"Yes, today is April third and you had a craniotomy a few hours ago."

"Didn't I have craniotomy surgery in March?"

"Very good, you remember. Yes, I took care of you then too. But four days ago, you came back into the hospital. Today, they did another craniotomy to remove more fluid." She picked up a non-contact thermometer and held it in front of his forehead before returning to the cart and entering more data.

That was one piece of the puzzle, but it did not reduce the fog by much. He racked his brain and had a vague memory of having to return to the ER. *How many of these craniotomies have I endured?*

"When was my first craniotomy?"

"That was the twenty-third of March."

He struggled to think clearly, but it seemed important to know what happened during the missing time. He thought long and hard. "But that was many days ago, right?"

"Eleven days ago."

Why can't I remember the past eleven days? What happened during that time?

"Is this my *second* brain surgery, or have there been others?"

"This is number two and hopefully your last." She inspected the IV bag hanging on the pole next to the bed and made an adjustment to the regulator.

"Can you help me call my wife?"

The nurse turned to Chris with a smile. "When you first got out of surgery, Dr. Matthews visited, and you were on FaceTime with your wife. You might not remember, but you did talk to her a little. She was happy to see you."

He had no recollection of talking to her or Dr. Matthews, but he did not let the nurse know. Better to sit on that information until he could decide if it was a problem or not.

"I can't roll over. Can you help?" He was extremely uncomfortable on his side.

"I'm sorry, but we have you propped up with pillows in order for gravity to help the drains work better."

Ah, that explains it. At least I'm not paralyzed.

Moving around to the other side of the bed, she adjusted the pillows. "There, maybe that will help. You'll have to remain in bed for a while. They want to give your brain time to recover from the surgery. In addition to the two drains, you have a urinary catheter and an IV. Are you in any pain?"

"No. I'm okay. Sleepy."

"It's good to rest." She laid a heavy cloth over his eyes. "That should block out the light. Do you want earplugs?"

"Uh, no. It's not as loud in here as last time."

"We moved you to the quietest spot we could find. If you need anything, here's my call button." She made sure he could feel the button under his finger. "I'll be back to check on you."

"Thank ... thank you." He felt very sleepy, but he didn't want to give in yet. He wanted to figure out as much as he could.

He began listening carefully and heard the rhythmic hissing sound of ventilators around him. He had learned what ventilators sounded like after his first surgery when they had been all around him. It wasn't a sound he could easily forget. Whoosh, then a motor humming, and little irregular beeps.

I'm thankful I don't have to rely on a machine to breathe. And that I only had two brain surgeries. Must have turned out okay. I'll call Amy ... when I wake up. I'm so tired.

April 4

Chris awoke and tried to get his bearings. There was something heavy across his eyes and he reached up to touch it. *Oh yeah, the nurse put that there to block out the bright lights.* Shoving it off, he looked around. He fumbled with his phone and eventually was able to FaceTime Amy.

She answered right away. "Oh, I'm so glad you called. I was just wondering if it would be okay to call you, but I didn't want to wake you up too early. How do you feel?"

He immediately felt better at seeing her gorgeous face. "I feel good. I haven't gotten out of bed yet. I'm kind of stuck. I'm propped on my side so the drains can work better. I have a catheter and an IV, so they've got me coming and going." He rolled his eyes.

She giggled. "Oh, that's funny. You're already making jokes. I can't believe it. Do you remember much from yesterday?"

"I can't remember much of the past few days."

"When they came to get you for surgery, you couldn't talk or move your right side at all. They had trouble keeping you awake. The nurse had to get permission from me over the phone for the surgery because you couldn't even do that. It's a miracle you're talking to me now. And *you* called me. That's amazing." Her voice quavered.

Was I really that bad off? "I guess it's a good thing they decided to do surgery when they did. I've been trying to figure out what happened to me, but nothing at all comes to mind. It's like the door was shut, nobody home." He paused. "I don't even know who I'm talking to now, eh. But she sure is good-looking, don't ya know."

"Oh, stop it." She giggled.

He relaxed a little. If she was laughing, the surgery must have gone well.

"So how long do I have to stay in here this time?"

She immediately sobered up. "A few days. They need to monitor you carefully. We don't want this to happen again."

"No. Definitely not." He didn't like how serious she sounded. "Tell me the truth—how bad was it? I mean, will I recover or ..."

"You were pretty bad. But I believe you will recover fine." She gave him a small smile. "I have *faith* you will recover. I miss you, and I can't wait till you come home again."

"Me too." Food services walked in with his food tray. "Oh, gotta go."

"Okay, babe. I love you."

"Love you too."

He cringed at the smell of the dish in front of him. He certainly didn't have an appetite, but he'd do anything to get strong and go home. He buzzed for the nurse to help him sit up.

Amy talked to Chris several more times as the day passed, and each time he sounded better. He still couldn't remember anything since the last time he was in the hospital, which both concerned and relieved her. She was relieved he might not recall their terrible fight, but she didn't want him to lose his memory.

She took on other neglected cleaning projects around the house, blasting her music, singing, and pausing to dance occasionally.

She stopped for an update from Dr. Matthews.

"Your husband didn't have a run-of-the-mill hematoma. The quick regrowth of the membrane remnants and excessive fluid is highly unusual."

Her heart raced. "Do you ... do you know what's wrong with him?"

"Not yet. I'm glad I sent the sample to pathology. Today, I got word that there was some suspicion of an infection in the tissue sample. So, I asked a neuropathologist from a sister hospital to look at it too. I think an extra pair of eyes might help us unravel the mystery. It will be several days before we hear back."

She paused from scribbling notes. "What kind of infection? Is it ... could it be fatal?"

"I don't think so, but we need to figure out exactly what it is. In the meantime, I'm encouraged he continues to improve, and his drains are both putting out a fair amount of fluid. He is being given a full course of antibiotics as well. Daily CT scans will keep track of the brain's return to a normal position. There will be good days and bad days— that is totally normal for this type of surgery. And it could be a year before he is fully recovered. But we can expect things to go much more smoothly from here on out. I'm happy with the progress he has made."

She blew out a breath. "Thank you so much, Dr. Matthews."

After the call, she worried Chris had some mysterious infection and was glad they were already giving him antibiotics. As she thought about it, Dr. Matthews didn't sound concerned. If it were that serious, he wouldn't have been so encouraging about Chris's progress.

With each passing hour, she felt more optimistic. Surely the worst was behind them now. Soon her husband would be home, and they could make up properly once she confessed to him about her failures in their marriage. *I can imagine how sweet our reunion will be.*

Suddenly, she felt ravenous. She hadn't been eating much since Chris had gone back to the hospital. She decided to make a takeout run to Tabikh. After calling in her order, she jumped in his Hellcat. He would be happy she took Jezebel out for a spin. How many days had it been since she had driven anywhere? It felt strange to see streets empty of traffic.

She approached the door but realized she had forgotten her mask in the car. She turned back to retrieve it, then entered the café. The aromas were still as appealing as ever, but the tables were all empty. Chairs were placed upside down on top of them and the lights had been dimmed. Would the little café survive the pandemic on take-out orders alone?

She spotted Isra in the kitchen. "Hi, friend."

"It's great to see you." Isra came around the counter and stood a respectable distance away. "How are you and Chris doing?"

"Well ..." She wondered where to start. "You probably haven't heard, but Chris is in the hospital for the second time in a couple weeks."

"Oh no. I didn't hear. I am out of the loop. Is it the virus?"

"No, thankfully." She filled her friend in on the details.

"Oh my, this is incredible. I'm sorry to hear this. How is he? Were you able to be there with him?"

"Thanks. It's been a nightmare. I was with him for the first surgery, but not this last time. I can't believe all this is happening during a pandemic. Of all the inconvenient times to get sick. It's been quite a ride."

She filled Isra in on the rest of the medical details, and by that time Elias had joined them. He was as shocked as his daughter about Chris's recent health scare. His sorrowful face almost made Amy burst into tears. She wished she could hug both of her friends, but it was too risky. She had to make sure she was healthy for Chris to come home. They stood at a distance and waved as she left the café, the smell of their tasty food and loving wishes warming her heart. They offered their help with anything she needed. It was wonderful to have great friends at a time like this.

A few days after Chris's second surgery, Amy found herself once more on the roller coaster ride as his initial improvements had reversed into a troubling cascade of baffling complications.

When she talked to him, there were times when he recalled he had brain surgery and times when he couldn't remember what day or time it was. When she checked on him, most of the time the nurse said he was sleeping. When they did speak, his speech was garbled, especially in the mornings. Dr. Matthews said this was called expressive aphasia and was not uncommon in brain surgeries. He assured Amy it should only be temporary.

The doctors continued to test for possible reasons for the change in his speech. On the chance the expressive aphasia might be something other than brain irritation, they did an EEG to check for seizures. But the test showed nothing.

They did an MRI to look for a stroke, because Chris still had weakness in his right arm. Again nothing.

Since he had not been mobile for some time, they got him up and moving around to lower the risk of a lung infection. And they did a chest X-ray. All clear.

His white blood count had been high but was now falling, so that seemed to rule out an infection. Yet his temperature was quite high, and they were using IV antibiotics to treat what they had to assume was some form of yet-undetected infection. Either the fever or the cocktail of medications—or both—could have caused him to be less coherent.

Dr. Matthews called her daily, giving updates and reassuring her. "This is an unstable period, partly related to removal of the drains, the fever, some of the meds, and the cumulative effects of being sedentary in the hospital for more than a week."

Amy felt extremely frustrated because she couldn't talk to Chris or see him. When she did get to speak to him, she was alarmed at how he struggled with words. He clearly wanted to talk and made plenty of sounds, but she had trouble piecing together what he was saying. For his sake, she acted as if she was following along with whatever he said.

What a change from the past years of conflict when she understood every word but acted as if she was interested in none of it. Would he ever be himself again? She sobbed for hours every night, her mind spinning with what-ifs and if-onlys. But there was no going back, no matter how bleak the future seemed.

April 8. Morning

Outside Amy's bedroom, the sun had begun its trek across the Northern Hemisphere, oblivious to the McGraths' plight. The warming rays splayed across her bed, waking her up.

She got out of bed slowly, feeling as if she had aged ten years in a matter of days. She shuffled downstairs to look for some breakfast. Opening one cupboard after the other, she saw nothing that looked appetizing. In the refrigerator, she found one last yogurt. She got a spoon and sat down to eat.

Would she get to talk to Chris today? The last three days they'd not been able to speak at all. She worried about what he might think. *Does he wonder why I'm not calling him? Does he realize I've tried so many times? What is going on in his mind?*

She spent a lot of time each day communicating with friends and family members. The kids were terrified for their dad, and Amy had tried to reassure them. Once again, she felt thankful they were with family even if they couldn't be with her.

She went upstairs to get dressed, but only stood in front of her closet staring. *Maybe I'll just stay in my pajamas today.* It took more energy than she had to brush her teeth and get dressed. She was terrified not knowing if Chris would ever be the same. She prayed desperately, and she knew a lot of people were praying for him. But ... what if God didn't answer the way they wanted him to? Losing him—even mentally—felt too overwhelming to her. All she wanted was to have a chance to make things right and be the kind of wife she should have been all along.

But as the days went by, she felt a tremendous struggle to stay positive.

She hadn't finished her cleaning tasks, but lost interest in housework. Worrying took up most of her time and there wasn't margin for much else.

Her mom and sister cooked meals for her and brought them every couple of days. They would sit on the lanai in their winter coats, a roaring fire in the fireplace. She relished these moments with her loving family. What would she have done without them?

The word had spread about his hospitalization and many people wanted to help in some way. She would often get a text out of the blue ...

DANNA: There's something for you on your porch.

She would discover the most delicious treats—cheese-stuffed pasta shells, homemade cookies, baklava.

One talented friend came for a porch visit and brought along her ukulele, playing and singing "You Are My Sunshine."

A neighbor she had never met came over with her two small children. They had cut out construction paper hearts in many colors and taped them to her front window like a rainbow.

She was constantly amazed at the kindness of people she barely knew. *Maybe they've always been as kind. I'm finally recognizing it because my heart is softened.*

One morning, she silently cried as she sipped her morning coffee. Even though so many people had reached out to encourage her, the reality was that Chris's health was still mysteriously compromised, and they were still separated by a terrifying pandemic. The sun was shining outside, but her heart was blanketed in darkness. Her phone rang, and she jumped to answer it. Dr. Matthews's PA was calling. Was it more bad news?

"Good morning. Chris is awake, his eyes are open, and he is following commands better. Would you like to FaceTime with him?" Her friendly, positive voice instantly infused Amy's heart with hope.

"Oh yes, I would!"

As his face came into view, she put on a big smile. She missed him so much and yearned to connect with him. She told him a couple of funny stories, and he chuckled a bit at them. She was delighted he was aware the stories were supposed to be funny. He didn't respond much verbally, but he seemed to be tracking cognitively. He looked like he was going to cry a couple of times. She wished the PA could just stand there all day holding the phone, but that wasn't realistic.

"Chris, make sure you eat all the food they give you, okay? Maybe today you will get to move to the rehab floor, and after that you can come home. Would you like that?"

He responded with a few grunts and a few mumbled words.

She worried about him being in the hospital so long without connection to loving family members and caring friends. *He must feel alone. What is going on inside his head all day long? He doesn't even have a TV.* She gave him some news from their parents, the twins, and their friends. He typically enjoyed hearing what everyone was up to. She hoped that was true now. He seemed to recognize familiar names, but she couldn't tell if he understood the details about them.

"I love you, Chris." She wanted most of all to reassure her husband of her love. Her affection for him had been building inside her to the bursting point. Their past conflicts had completely melted away, and nothing mattered to her but loving him with all her heart.

The PA helped Chris respond. "Chris, say 'I.'"

He repeated, "I."

"Love."

He stumbled over that word, and it came out "Like."

"You."

He was able to say "You." They all laughed at that.

Amy made a joke about it. "I like you *too*."

They shared eye contact and grins. That would have to be enough for now.

She decided to spend some time listening to God that afternoon. She could use some encouragement. She settled herself on the sofa, Bible in her lap, and began thinking about God.

Will you give me a picture of how you see Chris now? I can't see him, but you can.

In her mind, she saw Chris sleeping in his hospital bed. In the distance, a huge, brilliant white bird flew toward him. It gently settled down next to where her husband lay and unfurled an enormous wing to wrap around him. He looked so tiny under the wing, but also safe and warm. Then she saw the bird unfurl its other wing, and it reached out to her sitting on the sofa. The wing covered her, snuggling her close to its soft side and beating heart. The colossal wing was inches from her face, but she couldn't see any feathers. She was so close the image seemed pixelated.

What an amazing picture. It comforted her to think God was not only with her, but with Chris at the same time.

She felt refreshed after her quiet time and decided to call Chris and at least try to explain what God was doing in her heart. She believed he would be interested even if he didn't know what to say in response. Maybe he would relate to that beautiful picture of comfort.

The call rang several times before going to voice mail. "Hi, Chris. Can you call me back or ask a nurse to call me on your phone? I wanted to hear your voice. I love you."

As she disconnected the call, she wondered if his battery was dead. She decided to try the room phone. She punched in the number and waited.

She let the phone ring a long time. She knew it was hard for him to reach the phone on the small table next to him. There was a plethora of equipment, and he couldn't move fast. Finally, she ended the call, hoping she hadn't disturbed him. *I'm sure he's just resting. At least I hope so.*

April 8. Evening

An hour later Chris still hadn't called her back. As she scrambled to find the number for the nurses' station, her phone rang.

"Mrs. McGrath, this is Nurse Angie. I was your husband's nurse a few nights ago. I wanted to let you know we have received a release to move your husband to the fourth floor. Dr. Matthews believes he will improve with some therapy. We did get him up and walking about twenty feet earlier today. He still is unable to say much, but we are hopeful this move will do him good. We will call you as soon as he is settled in. The room number will be 4440."

"That's great news. Thank you, Angie."

"Would you like to say hi to him now? We probably have a few minutes before the orderly comes."

"Sure."

Angie switched to FaceTime and held the phone so Amy could see her husband.

Chris was sitting up in bed, and he looked alert, although he wasn't smiling. Nevertheless, she was delighted to see his face again. "Hi. It's good to see you. Did you hear the news?"

"Yeah."

"You're getting moved to a new room, and you will be going to physical therapy. Isn't that awesome?"

"Yeah."

Her heart sank that his expression didn't change, and she couldn't read what was going on with him. His voice sounded hollow. She kept smiling and tried to sound lighthearted. "I'm sure you will do well and impress the physical therapists. After you get settled in your new room you can tell me how you like it, okay?"

"Yeah."

"I love you."

"Yeah."

Angie turned the phone around. "Sorry to interrupt. They are here now to move him. Someone will call you as soon as he gets settled in."

"Thank you, Angie. You have no idea how wonderful it is to see his face."

She disconnected the call and hugged her knees to her chest. Finally, some progress. She turned on music and danced around, picking up the glasses and dishes that sat on virtually every horizontal surface.

About a half hour later, the phone rang again.

"I'm sorry, but we won't be moving your husband after all," Angie told her. "As they were raising the bed to transfer him, he had a small seizure. It was what we call a focal seizure, involving only his right cheek. Immediately after that, he went unresponsive for several moments. When he woke up, we asked him the normal post-seizure questions. We also called in the neurologist for further consultation. He is sleeping soundly now, but his fever is 101.3. There haven't been any more seizures. Don't worry, we will be watching him closely."

Amy didn't reach for her notebook or pen, she just slid down to the floor. *When is this torture going to end? Another setback? What is happening?*

"What kind of questions did you ask him?" It was the only thing she could think of to ask.

"We normally ask who, what, when, and where types of questions. Since your husband can only say the word 'yeah,' I asked him if he knew what his name was. He answered 'yeah.' I also asked him if he knew what day it was and if he knew where he was. Both times he said 'yeah.' But we're unsure if he truly does know those things or if he just feels he must answer, and 'yeah' is all he can say."

"Oh ..." Amy's voice trailed off.

"Dr. Matthews wanted you to know he will call you later today. Do you have any questions?"

"No. Thank you. I appreciate you calling me back."

"I will be here for the rest of the shift. Please call me if you think of anything."

Amy sat on the floor against the wall trying to muster up the energy to move. Terrifying scenarios played in her mind. Didn't seizures cause brain damage? Would his personality change? What if he never returned to the old Chris she knew? What caused the seizure? Would there be more? Suddenly a revelation broke through the terror. *Wait a minute. I don't have to give airtime to worries that may never come true. I can choose to let go of worry and trust God instead.*

She moved to the family room sofa and switched on the TV. Searching the YouTube channel, she found exactly what she wanted—the long video of a fireplace. The peaceful sound of a crackling fire and the mesmerizing scene of the dancing flames were perfect for her now. As she gazed at the sight, she settled in for the wait ahead of her, breathing in the peace and quiet. She bowed her head and prayed.

She was startled when her phone rang an hour later. She grabbed her notebook and pen.

"Hello, Amy, it's Dr. Matthews. I wanted to call you as soon as I could. Chris's partial seizure was short, only involving his face, and he was unresponsive for a short while afterward. There haven't been any others since then. He is weary now, which is normal after a seizure. His temperature is down to only 98.9 and the highest today was 101.3. The neuropathology report came back, which indicated there was an infection in the membrane we sent to the lab. They were not able to be absolute in their conclusion, but the report points to a type of infection called a subdural empyema, a pocket infection."

"Wait—I'm trying to write all this down. How do you spell that infection?"

Dr. Matthews spelled it slowly and gave her a moment before he continued.

"It's relatively rare. In the meantime, the infectious disease doctor has prescribed three different antibiotics, and we will install a PICC line to feed him the IV antibiotics because he will be on them for an extended duration."

Amy paused her writing. "Pick line? What's that?"

"Sorry, that's a peripherally inserted central catheter. A PICC line is a long, thin catheter tube that will be inserted through a vein in his arm and passed through to the larger central veins near his heart. It's better than an IV for long-term injections of medicines and can help avoid the pain of frequent needle sticks."

Amy continued documenting all the doctor said. "Are you sure he didn't have a stroke? I'm not an expert, but I'm concerned he can't talk."

"We performed an MRI, which was negative for a stroke or new areas of bleeding. But the brain must still be irritated in the regions where speech and the upper right side motor functions are controlled. The seizure isn't an unusual development, either. He just needs more time to recover and heal. The antibiotics will do their job quickly, and I believe he will recover soon."

"Okay, thank you for all your time, Dr. Matthews."

After the call disconnected, she went back to studying the fireplace until her text notification went off. She looked at her phone and saw Dr. Matthews had texted her.

DR. MATTHEWS: Don't worry.

She said a prayer for Chris's doctor then. She needed to remember to pray for this amazing doctor more often.

After hours of watching nothing but a crackling fireplace on the TV and now the doctor's update, Amy yawned deeply. One more call to Nurse Angie to check on her husband and she would head up to bed.

"Hi, Angie. I just wanted to check to see how Chris is doing."

"I'm right here with him. He's been asleep most of the time since I talked to you last. You spoke to Dr. Matthews, right?"

"Yes, I did a couple of hours ago. Has Chris been stable since then?"

"He has. Every time I check on him, he is sleeping, as he is now. His temperature was 98.9 the last time I checked." She paused for a moment. "Oh ... he just had another seizure. It was a short one, just affecting his facial muscles. Oh ... and there's another one." Her voice sped up. "I must hang up now. I need to call Dr. Matthews. We'll be in touch."

Amy crumpled into a ball and clutched a throw pillow. *No, it can't be. What if I never get a chance to tell him how sorry I am for my part in our struggles? What if his brain doesn't heal enough to understand me? Or ... or what if he never comes home?*

She felt utterly helpless and sobbed loudly until she was spent. Then she just lay there, feeling numb and frozen. While her mind wandered, she vividly recalled the image of the heavenly bird holding her and Chris securely to its soft, comforting chest. Peace seeped into her battered heart, and she found herself breathing evenly again. God was still holding them close to his heart. He would never let go. He was taking care of Chris right now even when all hope seemed lost.

She desperately needed to talk to someone. She got up, washed her face, and found her phone.

Linda picked up at once. "Oh, I'm so glad you called. I've been feeling a heaviness as I prayed for you. How's Chris?"

Amy filled her in on the latest distressing details. Speaking them out loud made her realize how dire Chris's situation was.

"Oh, Amy, I'm so sorry. All these setbacks—especially the seizures—are very upsetting. I'm sure I've said this about a thousand times already, but I would be there to give you a hug if we weren't all quarantined from the pandemic."

"It's awful. The ups and downs are exhausting, and I feel so helpless. I don't know what's going to happen."

"I can't even imagine."

"I'm having an extremely hard time. Nothing I've ever faced has been as difficult. At times I can't handle it and break down. I know I should be strong and hold it together—"

"Amy, stop. That's not true. You're human, and you can only handle so much. You are going through an extremely traumatic situation. It's not healthy to try to stuff it all down and act strong. Let your emotions come out. Turn to God when you feel weak. Be gut honest with him about everything you feel. He will comfort you."

"I ... well, it's hard. I've always been able to tough out every situation. Being weak and helpless is new for me. Thank you for letting me know it's okay." She blew out a cleansing breath. "And yes, I've been turning to God since I am all alone and can't get out and see other people. He is incredibly comforting to me. He is never confused or frightened or unsure like I am. Even though I adore Chris above all else, *God* loves him even more than I do. That gives me peace, even in all this turmoil."

"Oh, honey. I'm so glad to hear that. Through the worst times in my life, I clung to the Lord. He held me up, comforted me, and carried me when I couldn't go any further on my own. I'm so grateful to hear you are letting him do the same for you."

"Thank you so much for telling me how to listen to God. That's made all the difference for me. He recently gave me the most reassuring visual."

"Really? Do you feel comfortable sharing it?"

"Definitely. The booklet said to confirm that the messages we receive are biblical, so I'm really interested in your opinion."

She took a deep breath, let it out slowly, and closed her eyes. Then she related to Linda how God gave her the picture of holding both Chris and her under his wings, close to his heart.

"Hmm," Linda started slowly. "I can think of many ways Scripture confirms it. God's wings are mentioned in the Bible often, especially in giving us shelter from the storms of life. He is everywhere at the same time, which explains the bird's wings touching both you and Chris simultaneously." Linda's voice dropped to almost a whisper. "That is such a powerful and beautiful image. Would it be okay if I share it with Jim?"

"Of course."

After they ended the call, Amy stayed on the sofa. This time she wasn't numb and frozen ... she felt warmed and soothed.

April 9

Much earlier than normal the next morning, Amy received a call from Dr. Matthews. She was already awake since she hadn't slept much anyway. She opened her notebook and uncapped her pen as he gave his update.

"Throughout the night, I kept watch on him with a team of other doctors, including the neurologist and the specialist who is addressing his infection. The local facial seizures increased as the night wore on. His ability to speak and move his right arm continued to diminish. We started him off on a normal dose of an anti-seizure medication. However, the seizures continued, so we kept increasing the dosage and then added two stronger medications. Finally, near morning, the seizures stopped. But as is typical, the high dosage caused him to sleep heavily."

Amy was madly writing notes as she listened. "It's good the seizures stopped."

"Yes, it is good. Having seizures, even small ones like he was having, can cause permanent brain damage. However, as he got more and more sleepy, his breathing became labored. We decided to intubate him so a machine could breathe for him and give him a couple of days to rest comfortably so the antibiotics can go to work."

"What?" Her pen stopped in midair. "Do you mean you put him on a ventilator?" She had seen the apparatus on patients while watching the news. "The same equipment they are using for the virus patients?"

Dr. Matthews's calming voice reassured her. "Yes, a ventilator."

She didn't know what to say. She flipped back a few pages in her notebook. "I remember you told me he had a pocket infection called an empyema. Is that the infection you're talking about now, or is there another one?"

"Good memory. Yes, that's the infection I'm referring to. Remember that pathology could not be certain, but they believed the tissue sample could be an empyema, which is very rare. An empyema can be the result of a craniotomy or a sinus infection. It usually has a distinct color and is easy to visually identify. I didn't see anything that looked like an empyema during the first surgery, or I would have removed it. I saw in Chris's records he had been treated for a sinus infection several months ago. So, it is unclear if the empyema resulted from that sinus infection or a complication from the first surgery.

"What matters most now is he's being treated with several powerful IV antibiotics to stop the infection. We absolutely made the right choice in terms of a repeat surgery—he would never have gotten better through rehab."

"Uh … okay." She was still writing so she could do research later. "What's next?"

"Our plan is to keep him on the ventilator for two days, then gradually lower the anti-seizure meds. If all goes well, he should be down to just a maintenance level in several days. He is resting comfortably. They are giving him sedation so the tube in his throat is not bothering him. I will be in touch daily and my PAs will as well. My whole family is praying for him too."

"Thank you, Dr. Matthews. That's reassuring. This is a lot to deal with."

"I understand."

The call ended, and she fell to the floor in prayer. *Will Chris ever recover? Will he be able to think and talk and remember? Will we get a chance to make our marriage work? I have so many questions for you, Lord. And I know you may not tell me everything right now. I just need to know that he's going to be okay. Please?*

She remained on the floor for some time while she examined her heart and her emotions. The questions were there, as well as the uncertainty about his health and future.

Oh God, I'm so overwhelmed by everything. I know you have Chris and me under your wings. I firmly stand on that belief. I pray that you will spare his life and heal his mind.

She remembered the words she read in the Bible from the fourth chapter of 1 Peter early that morning. "The end of all things is near. Therefore, be alert and of sober mind so that you may pray. Above all, love each other deeply, because love covers a multitude of sins." *I forgive Chris for everything, Lord. Please forgive me for even more.*

After weeping silently for a while, she felt a calm assurance that God had heard her. She felt cleansed, forgiven, and strong again. She rose from her position on the floor and sang a soft song of thanksgiving and praise.

Feeling completely at peace now, she decided to write an update email to the members on Linda's prayer list. She had emailed them a few times when she had a significant update, and it was encouraging to read their responses. But when she went to her desk, she saw a note reminding her Linda and Jim had planned a Zoom meeting tonight. The prayer team had been praying virtually for her and Chris and had asked if Amy could join their next call. She craved any form of human connection and talking to these caring people was just what she needed.

She gasped when she saw the Zoom call was starting in two minutes, so she hurried to find the link and log on. It took her a few minutes to connect, then verify her video camera and speakers worked. The screen blinked and then came back on with eight faces looking back at her. She breathed a sigh of relief, unmuted herself, and greeted everyone with a wave.

Linda introduced them, and Amy remembered a couple of people from church. The rest were strangers, and it touched her deeply these folks were praying for her and Chris. One young man had a guitar with him, and he played and sang "The Lord Bless You and Keep You." She closed her eyes and focused on the reassuring words.

They asked her for an update, and she gave them the latest—the seizures, the ventilator, the uncertainty. But also, the hope.

A few people asked questions, and she answered them as best she could. She tried to put the names with the faces so that she could pray for each of these people as well.

When there were no more questions, she felt it safe to bare her heart. "God has done some amazing things throughout this whole time. Before this happened, Chris and I were having some relationship issues. It was like our marriage was on life support and only slightly healthier than his brain was. I thought everything was his fault, but I didn't see my own."

She stopped to take a deep breath, and a few people nodded. That made her feel supported instead of condemned. She continued with more confidence.

"It wasn't until he was hospitalized the second time that I began to listen to God and saw how I had misjudged my husband. Through this ordeal, I've learned I am completely helpless to change anything ... except myself. If—" Her voice cracked. "*When* Chris recovers, I will do my best to be the wife God wants me to be. Your prayers have been helping Chris, but you probably didn't know they also made a significant change in my life. I appreciate you all so much."

She had to wipe her eyes. Jim waited, then led them all in prayer for Chris's healing and full recovery. She wasn't the only person weeping by the end.

Then each person pronounced blessings and peace over them.

When the call ended and everyone was gone, she felt lighter than she had in a long time. A group of caring people were sharing her load. The multiplying boulders of stress, anxiety, and fear that weighed her down were gone. She was free.

April 10

The next morning, Dr. Matthews was making rounds and saved Chris's bedside for last, because he honestly didn't know what to expect. The events of the last several days had confounded him and his fellow physicians as they encountered one bit of bad news after the other. He remembered Chris presenting with a chronic subdural hematoma three weeks ago to the day. *I expected a run-of-the-mill evacuation with a quick return to normalcy. I had no idea what was up ahead for us all. Help me, God. I want to give them hope, but I don't know what today will bring. We need a miracle!*

As he stepped around the curtain, he saw Chris, eyes wide open and smiling—as much as possible with a ventilator tube in his mouth. He stopped in his tracks as Chris gave him a thumbs-up with his right hand. *Yes, he was using his right arm—the one he could not move for the last few days.* How could this be? But he was witnessing this sight with his own eyes. Unbelievable. He had never experienced a patient sink so far so quickly and then improve equally far and fast.

Chris had no idea how long he'd been sleeping, but he knew it was days, not hours. He had only wisps of memories.

A scene here and there. A swaying green curtain. The face of a nurse asking him questions he couldn't answer. They were always asking him those questions.

His most recent memory was of Dr. Matthews coming in to see him. He was awake enough to give him a thumbs-up sign, and Dr. Matthews mimicked the gesture with great enthusiasm. Doc did an examination and said he was extremely pleased with his progress. Chris tried to talk to him but had a tube in his mouth. *A ventilator?*

He must have fallen asleep after that. When he awoke, there was no tube down his throat. That was a good sign. His throat hurt, though, and he felt extremely thirsty. Groping around to find the remote, he hit the call button.

In moments, a nurse and the doctor's PA were beside his bed.

"Can you tell us your name?" The PA looked expectantly at him.

Of course, he knew his name, but his answer surprised himself. The sounds he produced were gibberish. He tried a few more times, each time speaking louder as if that would drive away the demonically garbled words. His name remained inside. No matter how he tried, he couldn't find a way to let it out.

The nurse brought him a small whiteboard. He picked up the marker and went to print his name. To his surprise, his hand wrote *HHHHH*. Frustrated, he erased it with his fist and tried again. Only *HHHHH* appeared. He studied the whiteboard for long minutes, afraid to try again. He looked up at the women next to his bed. *Can you help me?*

Neither woman batted an eye, but they looked positive and hopeful. The PA tried a different question. "Is your name Chris McGrath?"

"Yeah." *Now I'm making some headway.* It felt so good to answer at least that simple question. Both women apparently were encouraged and nodded their heads vigorously.

"Is your birth date February 14?"

He stopped, confused at the wrong date, then shook his head *no*.

The PA smiled. "Very good. Do you remember why you are here?"

"Yeah." Chris pointed to his head.

She spoke slowly and clearly. "Yes, that's right, you had a second craniotomy a few days ago. After surgery, you were having seizures. The medication to stop them made you overly lethargic. We had to place you on a ventilator to protect your breathing function. The doctor expected you to stay on it for two days, but you were able to get off in only one day."

"Yeah."

"Seeing you awake and thinking coherently is wonderful!"

That's good news. But why can't I talk or write? Will I ever be able to communicate again? What's happened to me? Panic seized his throat with icy fingers. What if he could only say "yeah" and motion with his hands from now on? It was a terrifying thought.

Wait a minute. Let me think ... He recalled Dr. Matthews saying he would have a full recovery. He remembered people were praying for him. Amy loved him and was pulling for him. He knew deep within his heart the Great Physician could perform miracles.

The icy fingers lost their stranglehold on his throat and slipped away.

It was almost as if the PA was able to understand his thoughts as she patted his shoulder. "We believe you will recover your former language and writing skills. In fact, you are already moving at a pace that is much faster than usual."

Those encouraging words spoken with such authority rang true to him. Chris accepted them as a gift.

He gave her a thumbs-up with his right hand.

She returned the thumbs-up.

He mimed drinking a cup of water.

The nurse spoke excitedly. "Oh, I'll get you some ice chips right away."

She left, and the PA said they would both be back to check on him.

Left alone with his thoughts, he tried to remember more about the last several days. There was a strong memory of feeling like he was falling, falling, falling—then crashing. And then nothing. That had happened several times. He tried to make sense of it. He couldn't ask anyone about it. He had to figure this one out for himself.

Did I die? I must have died. But I'm sure I am not dead now. Wonder filled him, and he felt certain he had somehow cheated death.

His thoughts turned to Amy. *Where is she? Does she know what is happening to me?* He couldn't remember the last time he saw her. Love for her throbbed in his chest. He wanted to talk to her, hold her, just be with her. For now, he had to be satisfied with being alive. The hope of being reunited with her kept him going. Tears gathered in the corners of his eyes, rolling down to his ears.

The song "Here Comes the Sun" began playing on the hospital speaker system. It brought fresh tears to his eyes thinking they might be playing that for him.

Thank you, God. His first prayer in a long time came from deep within his heart.

It was the middle of the day, and Amy sat on the front porch bundled up and enjoying the sunlight. Spring was her favorite time of year when life blossomed everywhere. Hope was blossoming in her heart today.

Early that morning, Chris's day nurse used FaceTime so Amy could see him. The ventilator was out now, a day early no less. He looked good. His voice sounded raspy from the ventilator, and she still couldn't understand a single word he said. Except for "yeah," that is. He answered in the affirmative to everything they asked him.

Isn't that just like him, the ultimate optimist? Hmm. That gives me an idea. She had wanted another puppy for years. She missed their dog who had died when the kids were still at home. But Chris didn't want another one, especially because of the freedom they enjoyed being empty nesters.

She got his attention. "I have a question for you. Are you ready?"

"Yeah."

"Now can I have a puppy?"

He vigorously and repeatedly shook his head no. He even managed to get out what sounded like "no." They all laughed. The old Chris was coming back.

Hours later, the nurse called her again. Chris wanted to talk with her. He still had an extremely low raspy voice, and most of the words he said were incomprehensible, but this time she caught a few he was struggling to articulate.

"No ... hello ... love you ... nurse ... doctor ... I can't ..."

He quickly ran out of steam and his voice faded as he struggled to stay awake. She reassured him they could talk again later and encouraged him to sleep.

"Yeah."

Amy sat for the longest time on the porch, reflecting on all the terrifying things they had been through in the last month. Who would have guessed back then how her love for him would have been kindled into such a blazing fire once again?

She remembered how Linda and Jim's relationship was healed when their marriage had been so fractured. Amy had been skeptical when she heard that, but now she could understand clearly. God *could* bring beauty from bad things.

A few days later, she was delighted to see how quickly Chris was regaining his ability to speak and move. The physical therapist said he was pushing himself hard to recover. He still wasn't out of the woods, but he was making steady progress. She was confident he could comprehend everything she said, even if he couldn't respond back. The doctor had reassured her that was the case. The irritation in his brain was only in the areas for output of communication, not in the input or comprehension areas. There hadn't been any more seizures, and his brain had begun the long process of restoration.

Today, she wanted to tell him what had been burning on her heart for so long. She called the nurses' station, and they were able to get him on his phone again. He began chattering away, his voice less raspy, wanting to tell her all about his adventures. Many of his words were still unintelligible, but she could catch so many more.

"Now I'm better ... Doctor Matthews ... seizure ... NO ... he says go home ... want to ... in the morning ... it's so nice ... he sings ... I love you ..."

She had to stop him from talking, or she wouldn't get a word in edgewise. "That all sounds wonderful. I can understand many more of your words now. But before you run out of steam, can I tell you something especially important?"

"Yeah."

"While you have been in the hospital, I've done a lot of praying. God is helping me to recognize how to love him and you as I should. I haven't done such a good job at that. I want to do better."

"I love you."

"I love you too." She paused and gathered her thoughts. "Linda taught me about listening to God. He speaks to us in our minds and in our imaginations. The other day God showed me a picture in my mind that really helped me when I was feeling lonely without you. I wanted to share the picture with you. Is that okay?"

"Yeah."

"I saw you in your bed in the hospital, and I was on the sofa at home. A huge white bird flew in and landed between us. He put his enormous wings around each one of us. The bird covered each of us and hugged us close to his side. Even though I couldn't be there with you, it made me feel close to you, because we were connected by the bird. I thought the bird was symbolic of God, because he is with you in the hospital and with me at home at the same time. Isn't that a wonderful picture?"

"Yeah."

"I love you so much. I am going to work hard to be the best wife I can be for the rest of my life. I can't wait for you to come home. So many people are praying for you, especially me. I know God is going to heal you and bring you back home to me soon."

Her voice became thick with emotion. She realized now how important words were. They can be life-giving and healing, or they can tear down and destroy. She hoped these words could heal some of the wounds her past words had caused. Chris remained silent for a moment. His sniffles were the only thing she heard.

"Are you okay?"

"Yeah ... very okay ... I love you ... much ..." His voice was slower and quieter. He was running out of steam.

But there would be time later for more talking and more healing. For now, this was good. She had a chance to gift him with life-giving words of affection. And that was all that mattered.

April 23

The day held much promise for Chris. Today, he would graduate from in-hospital rehab and go home. It had been twenty days since his second brain surgery.

But he was going home with a long list of medications, including IV antibiotics, which Amy would have to administer. She told him she was nervous about it, but he said he was desperate to return home, so she agreed to "morph into Nurse Amy." He was thrilled. He wanted her to take care of him—no one else.

Since being transferred to rehab, he had made steady improvement with help from physical, occupational, and speech therapies each day. The therapies challenged him, and they also made him realize how far he had declined. He was shocked at how little he was able to do at first. Shuffling twenty feet with a walker exhausted him. Simple addition problems were nearly impossible for him to decipher.

As he grew stronger, his cognition improved, and along with it, his desire to be out of the hospital and back at home also intensified. Not long ago, he had been content to stare blankly at a swaying green curtain. Now, he found himself getting frustrated with the endless waiting to be pronounced well enough to go home.

One bright spot was his ability to communicate, even if he was somewhat limited. He did this at every possible opportunity, mostly with Amy. But he also started tentatively texting friends and family. Typing only a few words would take fifteen to thirty minutes, but he worked diligently at the skill. But he wasn't confident enough to have a live conversation with anyone other than Amy yet.

Finally, the day arrived. He was overjoyed when his beautiful wife came into his room to take him home. He held out his arms to her. Dropping her purse and coat on a chair, Amy rushed to him and laid her head on his chest. They encircled each other in a long embrace. He breathed in the smell of her perfume and felt the comfort of her in his arms. They clung to each other, and he felt her body shaking. He felt like crying too. This had been the longest separation of their married life—thirty days in total, including the first brain surgery.

She helped him dress and packed up his belongings. They waited as each of the therapists came in to meet her and talk about next steps. Amy seemed overwhelmed with all the people and information, so whenever she'd look at him, he'd give her a thumbs-up or a wink.

Amy was handed a thick bundle of discharge instructions, a long list of medications, and several doctor appointments to keep. He was grateful that she'd keep track of it all. Then he watched her stiffen as a registered nurse showed her how to prepare an IV bag and hook it into the tube coming out of his PICC line. Would she be able to handle all this?

A steady parade of doctors, nurses, and aides stopped by to wish them well, and he and Amy thanked every single one.

Finally, they were in the car and ready to head home. He felt like he was getting away with something.

"Go! Make a ... break."

They both laughed as they drove away.

He relished looking out the window at the changing scenery. How long had it been since he was outside? He turned to look at her.

"What ... day?"

She replied, "What day is this? It's the twenty-third of April."

He continued to watch her, marveling at the way the sunlight lit up her face.

She glanced at him, and her head tilted to one side. "What are you thinking?"

"April twenty-third ... is special?"

She stopped at a traffic light, then turned to look at him. "Yes, it's my birthday today."

An ache of sadness filled his chest. "I have ... no ... present."

She gazed at him a long moment. "You are my birthday present, husband. There's no better gift for me."

When they pulled onto their street, Chris noticed cars lining each side of the street. As they approached their house, he was surprised to see a commotion. Parked cars crowded both sides of the street, masked people stood around everywhere—between the cars, on the sidewalks, and even in the middle of the street. As their car passed the people, they waved at him, jumped up and down, held up hand-painted signs, and shook pom-poms. Amy drove slowly down the street, car windows rolled down so they could hear the cheers.

A lump rose in Chris's throat. *These people all came out just for* me? He waved to everyone, struggling to hold back tears. It was so good to see his friends again.

He saw Isra and her dad, both waving wildly and cheering. Jim and Linda had pom-poms in their hands, crazily jumping around and cheering. Several people from church were there too. At the side of their driveway, Yo and Tamara held up a long banner between them that said: "We knew you could do it. Welcome Home, Warrior."

By the time they pulled in their driveway, he and Amy were both sobbing. What an amazing welcome home.

Amy's parents and Ronnie stood wiping their eyes on the front porch. Brad and Michelle also stood in front of the house, holding up their phones, recording everything. Next to them stood Carrie and Chris's mom Sharon, jumping and waving. Amy silently pointed to a man behind them holding a large sign that read "Welcome Home, Son."

Chris burst into tears. "It's ... my dad."

Amy turned to him. "Look at how blessed we are. All these people have come today to cheer you home. But they have also been cheering for us on their knees for weeks. All the time you were in the hospital, every day, they were supporting us and loving us and praying for us. They were our cheer squad, giving both of us the endurance to run this race. Where would we be without them?"

Chris felt completely overwhelmed as he wiped his eyes. She helped him put on his mask then put on hers as family members rushed the car to escort them inside.

The six days since Chris's homecoming had been a blur for Amy. She'd set up a chart to keep track of medication dosages, IV changes, and visits from the home healthcare team. Chris adjusted well to being home and expressed appreciation for every little thing she did. Little by little she was conquering her fear of administering the IV meds. They both took naps during the day, feeling exhausted at keeping up with everything, but they were together, which was a tremendous relief.

That afternoon, Chris said he felt good enough to have a video call with Jim and Linda. Excited, Amy coordinated the call. As they chatted, they all rejoiced in what God had done in the past month. Not just the medical miracles for Chris, but also the miracles in their marriage. Amy said the changes were due to all Jim and Linda had done for them.

Jim quickly deflected the credit. "The real miracle in any healed relationship is the heart change in each spouse. You each came to the place where you were willing to take a good long look in the mirror and tell God the truth about the wrong path you had taken. That's all he asks of us—to admit how lost we are. Then he simply leads us back to the right path, no judgment."

She felt Chris tugging her sleeve. She waited patiently as he struggled to articulate his words. "We were apart ... and we were scared ... and God made us better."

Linda nodded. "You're right. Sometimes our suffering is difficult, but it brings us to the place where we are willing to ask God for help. We let go of our need to be in control. When we think we may lose someone, suddenly the petty things we argued about seem irrelevant, and we are willing to let God change us to restore the relationship."

Amy still wanted to acknowledge their mentors' role in their healed marriage. "Those are good points. But God also used both of you, not to mention the wonderful prayer team. You all had a significant part in this process."

Jim replied, "For sure, Amy. Here's an analogy. I don't know if you've ever seen the giant sequoia trees in California. They're amazing. We learned that they could weigh five hundred tons and grow something like three hundred fifty feet into the air, yet their roots only extend six to twelve feet into the ground. Doesn't that seem incredible? Why would God design them that way? Seems like they would be vulnerable to falling. But we learned they seldom blow over in a storm. The secret lies in the fact that sequoias grow close to one another, and their root structures are locked together into a tight weave that gives them powerful support."

Amy loved that visual. "How cool is that? And what a picture of people locking arms together to support each other." She turned to look at Chris. "We are now a part of this support system. Who knows what might come of this episode in our lives? Maybe we will even become mentors someday."

"Yeah."

They all had a good laugh, but she was not kidding. Amy felt compelled to go deeper in terms of what they had been talking about. She had learned her lesson about holding back and risking the opportunity to say it at all.

"I realize the real disaster wasn't Chris having two brain surgeries or that they occurred during the pandemic. It was our fighting each other. The surgeries, setbacks, time apart, and complete helplessness exposed the selfishness in our hearts. We both turned to God, and he softened us toward each other. It's amazing how God can take even terrible situations and use them for our good if we let him."

Chris squeezed her hand tightly while Jim and Linda said, "Amen."

When Love Embraces Oneness— A Few Months Later

A few months after Chris returned home, he and Amy went away for a weekend to a cabin in the woods. They savored the beauty of nature and simply being with each other. They watched virtual church services together. They lingered over delicious meals and fell asleep in each other's arms at night.

He learned a lot about his time in the hospital from reading her journal and notebooks. He cried as he read through them and learned what had happened during some of the darkest days, many he had not been aware of. To experience even a portion of what she had to endure in her isolation and uncertainty was overwhelming. One part in her journal triggered a bittersweet memory for him.

He leaned back on the old leather love seat in front of a stone fireplace, stared at the flames for a few moments, then spoke. "Hey, babe, remember when you asked me if I was worried or afraid?"

She poked her head around the corner from the kitchen. "Yes. Why do you ask?"

"I said I was not afraid. But later, I thought more about your question. It helped me realize I wasn't *afraid*. I was *terrified*. When I asked God for help with my fear, he brought a ... a memory back to me."

Amy came and sat next to him.

"Do you remember when I went to the race car driving school in Arizona after we bought Jezebel? I can't remember the name of the school. That memory popped into my head when I asked God for help."

"Sure, I remember—the Bondurant Driving School. You loved that experience. How in the world did that help you overcome fear?"

He leaned back and smiled. "I remembered how cool it was riding along with the instructors. They were amazing drivers. One of the things I learned was the proper way to handle a skid. Most drivers feel terrified when they start skidding. They slam on the brakes or adjust too much with the steering wheel, and they spin out." He held his arms up and held an imaginary steering wheel, madly spinning back and forth. "The teachers explained why this happens. Most drivers are focusing on what is right in front of them. They become fearful, they overcorrect, and they lose control. The instructors said to keep our eyes focused farther down the road. The change in perspective helped us to minimize fear and make more subtle corrections. When we did that, a softer touch with the wheel or even the gas pedal did a better job of correcting the skid."

She tapped her chin. "I get it. When we stay focused on our immediate problems, our fear can easily spin out of control. But when we keep our perspective on heaven, the fear becomes more subtle and won't overwhelm us."

"Exactly. I believe God was telling me to look farther down the road and trust that I was in his hands. My terror vanished. I was okay whether I was healed or not. I almost called you back to tell you that. But at the time, I wasn't ready to be vulnerable with you, especially not from a hospital bed."

She hugged a pillow to her chest. "I can relate to that."

He reached out and took her hand. "Seriously, I want to be more open with you. Starting now. I've thought about how you reacted to the Bible study I did with Jim. I shared *my* feelings with you, but I never acknowledged *your* hurt at being left out. Your feelings were justified, and I want to apologize and ask for your forgiveness."

"That means so much to me. I do forgive you. And I owe you apologies as well. While you were in the hospital, I was desperate to feel connected to you, so I read through your notes in the Bible study workbook. I'm sorry I read them without your permission."

"They were thoughts I wished I could have said out loud. I'm glad you read them."

"The notes helped me understand your pain. I realized for the first time how my attitudes and words made it hard for you to be open." She paused and looked away. "You're not the only one who struggles with being vulnerable. I do too." She turned back to him, looked into his eyes, then eagerly described how Jesus showed her that oneness in marriage was a journey toward a common destination. Their journeys were uniquely designed for each of them by their Creator. As they grew closer to him, they grew closer to each other.

He rubbed her hand with his thumb while she was talking.

"Will you forgive me for being critical of you when you didn't follow the path *I* had in mind for you?"

"Of course." He remained silent for a few minutes, then slid off the love seat and onto his knees on the floor. He turned and offered his hand to her. "Will you pray with me?"

Amy took his hand and knelt next to him.

"God, we are overwhelmed by how good you have been to us. We have a long way to go, but we know you will be with us on this journey to oneness. We want to be able to give back and help other couples someday. Please help us to do that." He turned to look at his wife, waiting for her to add to the prayer.

"What he said. Amen."

They embraced each other as they sat on the floor. The dancing flames of the fireplace reflected the fire of passion and devotion in their eyes. They stayed that way for a long time, intertwined like the sequoia trees by their deep love for God and each other.

Afterword

Imagine your spouse is suddenly stricken with undiagnosable headaches and must ultimately be rushed into surgery. Because of COVID-19, you can't even go into the hospital. Then a second surgery is necessary. Specialists are baffled. You don't know if your beloved spouse of forty-four years will survive. The isolation, trauma, and stress are unbearable. That's our story.

Bruce went through thirty days of hospitalization in March and April of the infamous 2020. His saga included two brain surgeries, seizures, intubation, loss of speech and right arm movement. He managed to avoid COVID-19 as the number of infected patients in that hospital system increased from 167 to 1,217. He returned home to me, and together, we worked through weeks of IV-delivered medications and months of therapy and recovery. We are grateful for his miraculous and complete recovery.

We thank God we both came through this life-altering event with our marriage, faith, and strength intact. However, many people go through terrifying health issues and overwhelmingly stressful situations every day. We wanted to share our story to encourage others that there *is* hope, no matter how bleak the situation seems! With God, *all* things are possible. That's the truth we want to infuse into discouraged, hurting hearts.

We started mentoring married couples at our church in 2012. Working with troubled marriages has increased from a side gig to our biggest and most important ministry since Bruce retired in 2019. We decided to fictionalize our story to illustrate how God can use challenges to heal marriages. *Love on Life Support* is Chris and Amy's fictional story, based on our personal medical story, our experience in mentoring couples with fractured marriages, and the unhealthy habits in our marriage before we made the commitment to follow Jesus. We wanted to illustrate the benefit of marriage mentors coming alongside a *love on life support* so that couples will pursue mentoring when needed. And perhaps couples with strong marriages will consider becoming mentors. Mentoring strengthened us and contributed to a blessed ending to our medical saga.

We hope no couple will experience a critical medical emergency like we did. But if you face a significant challenge, wouldn't it be great to have mentors and friends like Jim and Linda? The prayer team that supported us included mentors, mentees, Bible study groups, lots of loving family members, and many dear friends. Their prayer intervention on our behalf was the most significant factor in Bruce's miraculous healing.

Church mentoring ministries, marriage counselors, and great parachurch ministries like FamilyLife® are available to help couples work through relationship issues just like Amy and Chris experienced. If your marriage could use a tune-up, we want to encourage you to reach out for help soon. Sadly, most couples wait six or seven years. Why not breathe life into your marriage *before* it's on life support?

We felt compelled to tell our story. If one couple's love is resuscitated because of this novel, then it will be another way that our traumatic experience will have been used by God for good.

With prayers for you, dear reader,
Deb & Bruce Potts

About the Authors

Our story began in 1976, when we charged into marriage naively thinking we were in the driver's seat of life. By God's grace, he wooed us and called us to follow him after eighteen years of doing it on our own. Our greatest joy is sharing the wisdom God has given us about forgiveness, healing, and destiny, especially as it applies to marriage.

We're the proud parents of two married children and two amazing grandsons. We are living in Act II, aka retirement. Act II is where all the redemption, resolution, and especially the good ending happens. To keep us moving in Act II, we set a goal to hike ten miles in every state. We've completed thirty-five states so far.

We lead the Marriage Mentor team at the Orion, Michigan, campus of Kensington Church. We train other mentors, serve couples in crisis, and nurture a space where marriages can thrive in community.

Deb has been an inspirational Christian speaker since 2006. She's the author of *Making Peace with Prickly People: Transforming Relationships by Loving God, Self, and Others*. It includes a personality assessment and a downloadable study guide for small groups.

Deb also published *Mindful: Meditate & Color Your Way to Life-Giving Relationships*. It's a thirty-day devotional and companion to the above book.

Bruce has an undergraduate degree in Industrial Administration and an MBA from Wharton. He worked for forty-seven years in technology and start-up companies, primarily in the field of robotics. He spent a little more than half of that time as CEO and the rest as CFO. As a result, Bruce has extensive experience in public speaking. He's spent much of his life in the business world of the fictional character Chris from *Love on Life Support*.

We hope you have enjoyed reading *Love on Life Support*. We would be blessed if you would put a review on Amazon so that others will hear about it. For upcoming works and information on speaking engagements, visit www.debpotts.com.

Requests for information should be directed to: Deb and Bruce Potts, PO Box 80183, Rochester, MI 48308.

Made in USA - Kendallville, IN
15058_9781649497680
01.06.2023 1531